## Twelve . . . Going On Fifteen

"I'm a junior," Josh said. "I'm sixteen, too old for you."

Jessica felt her face grow hot. "Sixteen isn't too old," she said quickly. "I'm fourteen." Josh didn't look impressed. "And a half," she added. "Anyway, what difference does a year or two make?" Her heart was pounding furiously. If he only knew she was twelve, he'd double up laughing.

"Well," Josh said doubtfully, "I've never gone out on a date with a freshman before, but how would you like to be the exception to the rule? Are you busy this Saturday night?"

Jessica thought fast. Her mind was racing. She knew her parents would never consent in a million years. But that seemed easy enough. She just wouldn't tell them. . . .

Bantam Skylark Books in the SWEET VALLEY
  TWINS series
Ask your bookseller for the books you have
  missed

# SWEET VALLEY TWINS

# *The Older Boy*

Written by
Jamie Suzanne

Created by
FRANCINE PASCAL

A BANTAM SKYLARK BOOK®
TORONTO · NEW YORK · LONDON · SYDNEY · AUCKLAND

RL 4, 008–012

THE OLDER BOY
A Bantam Skylark Book / January 1988
4 printings through July 1988

Skylark Books is a registered trademark of Bantam Books, a division
of Bantam Doubleday Dell Publishing Group, Inc.
Registered in U.S. Patent and Trademark Office and elsewhere

Sweet Valley High® and Sweet Valley Twins are
trademarks of Francine Pascal

Conceived by Francine Pascal

Cover art by James Mathewuse

ISBN 0-553-15664-0

Published simultaneously in the United States and Canada

---

Bantam Books are published by Bantam Books, a division of Bantam
Doubleday Dell Publishing Group, Inc. Its trademark, consisting of the
words "Bantam Books" and the portrayal of a rooster, is Registered in
U.S. Patent and Trademark Office and in other countries. Marca
Registrada. Bantam Books, 666 Fifth Avenue, New York, New York 10103.

---

PRINTED IN THE UNITED STATES OF AMERICA

O       13  12  11  10  9  8  7  6  5  4

# The Older Boy

# One

◇

"Jessica, slow down!" Lila Fowler panted, roller-skating after her friend as fast as she could. Jessica Wakefield spun around with a giggle, her sun-streaked blond hair flying out behind her. The two girls were at the Sweet Valley roller rink, a very popular spot for middle and high schoolers. Jessica had just finished telling Lila about the adorable guy she'd met seconds earlier.

"Look at him," she said admiringly, watching Josh Angler skate around the circumference of the outdoor roller rink. "Lila, he's perfect. And I think he really likes me!"

Jessica and Lila had only been at the rink for half an hour, and Lila couldn't believe Jessica had already managed to have an adventure. "You have all the luck," she grumbled, leaning over to adjust her skates. "How come no cute older guys have come over to talk to *me*?" Lila's pretty face was screwed up in a scowl, and she wore that spoiled, why-can't-I-have-everything-I-want look.

Jessica and Lila were both twelve years old. They were in the sixth grade together at Sweet Valley Middle School. Neither of them had had much to do with boys, but Jessica was determined to meet someone older. Her twin sister, Elizabeth, thought she just wanted more adventure, but in truth Jessica was sick of being treated like a baby. And, as if someone had heard her thoughts, her wish was about to come true. Jessica met Josh when she was about to take a spill in the rink. Josh came up behind her at the last moment and steadied her. When she turned to thank him she found herself staring up at one of the cutest guys she'd ever seen. Blond wavy hair, broad shoulders, and the strongest tanned arms! They started talking, and before she knew what was happening she was flirting with him.

Lila still couldn't believe it. "He's too old for you," she objected. "I'm telling you, Jess. The second he finds out you're still in middle school, he'll skate off into the sunset."

"Who says he has to find out?" Jessica called out over her shoulder. With that she sped off, leaving an astonished Lila Fowler staring after her.

"Hey!" Jessica called, skating up to the spot where Josh was resting by the fence. She lowered her gaze a little and looked up at him from underneath her eyelashes, as she'd seen her favorite actress do in the movies. "I thought I'd lost you. You're such a good skater," she gushed.

Josh grinned down at her. He was *really* cute, Jessica thought. His dark brown eyes crinkled at the corners when he smiled. "You're not half-bad, yourself," he said. "Though I never would have guessed it since I practically had to scrape you off the ground before."

Jessica smiled. "Oh, I was just pretending to fall. I wanted you to catch me, that's all."

"No kidding?" Josh said. He looked hard at her. "You're cute, you know that?" he added.

Jessica tossed her hair over her shoulders and tried to look as if she were used to hearing this sort of thing. "Thanks," she said casually.

"In fact, you're *really* cute," Josh said, looking at her with growing interest. "Why haven't I seen you around at school? Are you a freshman or a sophomore?"

"Uh, a freshman," Jessica fibbed quickly. Luckily her older brother, Steven, was a freshman at Sweet Valley High, so she knew the names of a few teachers and had some idea of which classes freshmen took.

Josh looked disappointed. "I'm a junior," he said. "I'm sixteen, too old for you."

Jessica felt her face grow hot. "Sixteen isn't too old," she said quickly. "I'm fourteen." Josh didn't look impressed. "And a half," she added. "Anyway, what difference does a year or two make?" Her heart was pounding furiously. If he knew she was only twelve, he'd double up laughing.

"Well," Josh said doubtfully, "I've never gone out with a freshman before, but how would you like to be the exception to the rule? Are you busy this Saturday night?"

Jessica thought fast. She knew her parents would never consent in a million years. But that seemed easy enough—she just wouldn't tell them.

"No, I'm not busy," she said, trying hard to make it seem as if this happened to her all the time. "See that girl over there?" she asked, pointing across the rink at Lila. "She's one of my best friends. I'm staying at her house this weekend." Jessica made up her story as she went along. "Let me give you her address. You can pick me up there."

Josh looked doubtfully across the rink at Lila. "She looks kind of young," he said uncertainly.

Jessica changed the subject before he had a chance to reconsider. "Why don't we go to a movie or something?" She had read in the latest issue of *Ingenue* magazine that boys liked it when girls took an active part in deciding what to do on dates.

It worked. Josh seemed to forget about Lila. "A movie sounds fun. Maybe we can double-date with my best friend, Sam." He studied Jessica closely. "I still can't believe I haven't seen you around school. What classes are you taking?"

"Oh, the usual," she said airily. "Geometry, history, biology, English—you know."

Josh nodded. "Are you in any clubs? Do you

play a sport? I keep thinking I should have run into you before."

Jessica wished she didn't have to be so careful not to say something wrong. She didn't want Josh to think she was boring. The truth was that Jessica was always at the center of the action at school. She was on the Booster squad, a middle school cheering team, which mostly consisted of Unicorns. She was also a member of the Unicorns, a special club that prided itself on being super exclusive. The Unicorns loved being exceptional, which was why their favorite color was purple. Purple was supposed to represent royalty. Elizabeth thought they were snobs, but Jessica loved the club. Lila was a Unicorn, too. So was Jessica's close friend Ellen Riteman. But it seemed too babyish to tell Josh that sort of thing. The safest bet was to turn the conversation back to *him*. "What about you? Do you play a sport?" she asked.

Josh nodded. "I'm on the soccer team."

Jessica's blue-green eyes lit up. "I love soccer," she said. "Tell me more. What position do you play?"

Soon Josh was chatting easily about himself. Jessica felt that the ice had definitely been broken. She was annoyed when Lila skated up, a scowl on her face.

"Jessica, I want to go home," she complained. "We've been here for ages. I'm sick of skating."

"Go ahead. I'll meet you back at your house," Jessica said.

Lila looked miserable but didn't protest. When

she was safely out of earshot Jessica shook her head and turned back to Josh. "She's nice, but she's so immature," she confided.

Josh nodded. "Yeah, I can see that." Jessica felt her heart beat faster. She could tell Josh liked her. He certainly didn't put her in the same category with Lila.

She could barely wait until Saturday night. It was going to be her first honest-to-goodness *real* date. Not only that, it was with an older guy who could actually drive!

Now the only problem was working out the arrangements without her family finding out.

That evening the Wakefields had a casual barbecue supper out on the deck of their split-level ranch house. It was a nice warm night, and everyone was relaxing over hamburgers and cold soft drinks. Mr. Wakefield, a handsome lawyer, had changed from his business suit into a cotton sweater and khaki trousers. Jessica loved the way her parents looked. Her mom seemed so young, with her blond pageboy and blue eyes. She was so slim and pretty, people always thought she was the twins' older sister!

"I can't believe the circus is already sold out," grumbled Steven, the twins' fourteen-year-old brother. He set down the newspaper he'd been reading and pounded his fist on the table. Steven looked a lot like his father, with the same dark hair, dark eyes, and broad shoulders.

Elizabeth looked disappointed. "I wish we'd thought to get tickets earlier," she said. "I love the circus. Daddy, are you sure it's too late?"

Mr. Wakefield shook his head. "I hate to let you down. I should've thought of it earlier, too. Usually we order tickets in advance through the mail. Somehow it just slipped my mind this year. I'll keep my ears open at work, though. Maybe someone will want to sell some tickets."

The circus came to Sweet Valley only once a year, and it had always been one of the Wakefields' favorite events. It stayed in town only two weekends, though, and it seemed unlikely that tickets would become available. Ordinarily Jessica would have gone nuts over missing the circus, but she was too excited about Josh to care that much. All she could think about was Saturday night.

"Hey," Steven said, leaning over to rumple her hair, "you and Liz should be a circus act yourselves. You could call yourselves The Clones." He almost fell out of his chair, he was laughing so hard. "Get it— instead of clowns, clones?"

"Steven . . ." Mrs. Wakefield said reproachfully.

Jessica rolled her eyes. "Steven, you're such a baby sometimes. When are you ever going to grow up?" Her newfound maturity was making her see everything in a different light, including her older brother's antics. Steven always teased the twins about their identical appearance. It was true that on the outside they were almost completely alike. Both girls had long blond hair, blue-green eyes the shade of the Pacific Ocean, and dimples in their left cheeks. In fact, the only feature that distinguished them was a tiny mole on Elizabeth's right shoulder.

Elizabeth was four minutes older than Jessica, but sometimes those four minutes seemed like four years. Despite their identical appearances, the two girls had very opposite personalities.

Jessica adored adventure and believed that having a good time was the most important thing in the world. She loved being in the limelight and tended to get into more scrapes than she could handle. She often depended on her steadier, more reliable twin to come to her rescue, especially when it came to doing chores and homework. In spite of their differences, though, a special bond existed between the two girls, and they were best friends.

"Who's calling who a baby?" Steven said, looking at Jessica with a smirk on his face. Steven teased Jessica even more than he teased Elizabeth. In fact, he and Elizabeth often got together to tease Jessica. A favorite topic was her appearance. All Elizabeth and Steven had to do was to give Jessica a few strange looks, and she went crazy.

"Jessica's on a new kick," Elizabeth informed him. "She was telling me the other day that she wants to meet an older guy."

"Good heavens!" Mrs. Wakefield said. "Jessica, I hope you were kidding. Do you want me to get old before my time, worrying about you?"

Jessica decided this was a good time to change the subject. "It's really too bad about the circus," she said to her father. "Maybe Lila's father knows someone who can get tickets. And speaking of Lila, would you mind if I stayed over at her house on Saturday night?"

Mr. Wakefield was engrossed in a section of the newspaper. "Mmmmm," he said, only half-attentive to Jessica's request. "What did you say, darling?"

"I want to spend the night at Lila's," Jessica repeated. "You don't mind, do you?"

"Lila Fowler," Elizabeth grumbled, "is such a pain."

Jessica quickly forgot all about trying to act mature. "She's a lot better than Amy Sutton and Nora Mercandy and those nerds you hang out with!" she snapped, then turned back to her parents imploringly. "It's OK if I stay at Lila's, isn't it?"

"As long as Mr. Fowler doesn't mind, dear," Mrs. Wakefield said.

"Oh, he doesn't," Jessica assured her. The truth was that Mr. Fowler was going to be out of town for the next few weeks on business. In fact, he seemed to be out of town far more than he was home. Only the Fowler's housekeeper, Mrs. Pervis, would be there, but Jessica didn't see any reason to tell her mother that.

"Then it's fine. We should have Lila back here sometime, too. It's only fair," her mother added.

Jessica gave Elizabeth a smug look. Everything

was working out exactly the way she had hoped. Now all she had to do was invite herself over to Lila's for Saturday night so her date with Josh could take place exactly as planned!

# Two

◇

Jessica hummed cheerfully to herself as she opened the door to her closet. It was Saturday afternoon, and under ordinary circumstances she would have been tanning herself at the beach or hanging out at the mall with Ellen Riteman. But this was a special day. She had to decide what to wear on her date with Josh tonight.

Jessica had been over the plans with Lila at least a dozen times during that week. But, she just had to call once more to make sure Lila knew *exactly* what was going on. She went to the phone in the hallway and punched in Lila's number.

"Don't tell me it's you again," Lila groaned. Jessica could tell from the faint buzz in the background that Lila was talking to her from her cordless telephone. She was probably out by her big pool. "Jess, you're driving me crazy."

"Just let me go through it one more time. I'll be over at six-thirty to change clothes. Josh is picking me up in front of your house at seven-thirty. While I'm gone, if anyone calls, tell them I'm taking a bubble bath," Jessica instructed. "I'll be home by midnight at the latest."

"I know, I know," Lila said. "I'm supposed to leave the back-door key under the doormat and keep the hall light on downstairs. We've been through this, remember?"

Jessica sighed. "OK. Just remember not to breathe a word if anyone from my family calls."

Lila giggled. "I'm going to spy on you when he picks you up. I want to see what kind of car he drives."

Jessica's heartbeat quickened. She was sure Josh Angler would drive a really neat car—maybe even a Porsche. She hoped it was a convertible. She had a perfect image in her mind of the two of them speeding along, a full moon overhead, her blond hair sailing behind her in the warm breeze.

"What are you going to wear?" Lila asked curiously.

Jessica tugged the phone as far into her room as it would reach so she could inspect the contents of her closet. "Something really sophisticated," she said. "Hey, you know what would be perfect? You know that blue cotton dress Lizzie wore when she won that award for the special edition of *The Sweet*

*Valley Sixers?*" Elizabeth was the editor of the middle school paper. The dress Jessica was thinking of was very simple and elegant. She was sure it would make her look older, and would show off her blond hair.

"I bet Liz won't let you borrow it"—Lila laughed—"especially just to come over to my house and sit around all night."

Jessica frowned into her closet. Nothing looked right. The blue dress was the only answer! "Leave it to me, Lila," she said confidently.

That was the trouble with Lila Fowler, Jessica thought as she hung up the phone. She didn't have enough *imagination*. Of course Jessica wasn't silly enough to *ask* Elizabeth if she could borrow her dress. The thing to do was to sneak in while Elizabeth was downstairs helping their mother fold the laundry and snatch the dress off its hanger. By tomorrow it would be right back where she'd found it, and Elizabeth would never suspect a thing!

By six o'clock Jessica was ready. She had her overnight bag carefully packed, with Elizabeth's blue cotton dress folded neatly at the top so it wouldn't get wrinkled. She already had little butterflies in her stomach just thinking about what the evening would be like. For the dozenth time she checked her appearance in her bedroom mirror. She had decided not to wait for the last minute to put on her makeup, and she couldn't really tell in this light how it looked. Lila would know, she thought, opening her bedroom door and heading downstairs with her bag over her shoulder.

"Mom? Dad? I'm going over to Lila's now," she said, stopping out on the deck to say good-bye.

"Have fun, sweetheart. Be sure to thank Mr. Fowler for letting you stay over."

Jessica nodded. Mr. Fowler was in Tokyo! Luckily she would only have Mrs. Pervis, Lila's housekeeper, to worry about. And Mrs. Pervis let Lila do whatever she wanted.

"Jessica," Mrs. Wakefield said suddenly, putting down the interior design magazine she'd been reading, "are you wearing makeup?"

Jessica turned red. "A little. How does it look?"

Mr. Wakefield raised his eyebrows. "Makeup? Aren't you a little young for that?"

Jessica looked indignant. "I hardly have any on," she defended herself. "And it's very natural-looking, don't you think? All the girls in the Unicorn Club wear makeup. Ellen Riteman's even had a facial."

"Oh, dear," Mrs. Wakefield said. "Well, we can talk about this more another time. But I do think you look nicer with your face all clear and natural."

Mr. Wakefield nodded seriously. "I agree with your mom, Jess," he said fondly.

Steven, who had been listening to this exchange with suppressed glee, couldn't resist putting in his two-cents' worth. "Face it, Jess. The way you look right now, you could get into the circus without a ticket!"

"Steven!" Mrs. Wakefield said sternly.

Jessica felt tears spring to her eyes. "You all treat me like I'm about two years old," she snapped. "I happen to be twelve years old. I'm not a child anymore!" With that she spun on her heels and stomped off into the house again. Her nylon overnight bag bounced on her shoulder behind her.

She stopped in the powder room first and splashed cold water on her face. She didn't want to risk wearing too much makeup. She could start from scratch at Lila's house.

But one thing was for certain: *Josh* didn't think she was a baby. He believed that she was fourteen and a half—old enough to go out on a real date. And she fully intended to show him—and everyone else—that she was old enough to be taken seriously!

By seven-thirty Jessica was completely ready. "You look great," Lila said loyally. The blue dress was just right. With a pair of sandals to complete the outfit she looked sporty but elegant. Lila had helped her put her long hair in a French braid, and in the end just a few dabs of makeup had seemed sufficient. And Lila had lent her a matching straw handbag to put a few things in—some change, a handkerchief, and a purple change purse for good luck. "The Unicorns' color," Lila reminded her.

"Where is he?" Jessica demanded anxiously, pacing back and forth in front of the Fowlers' bay window. "He said seven-thirty, didn't he? Lila, do you think he's going to stand me up?"

"Nope! There's a blue sports car stopping," Lila exclaimed, pointing out front.

Jessica's heart pounded. This was it. She was really going out on a date! "Wish me luck," she said, leaning over and hugging Lila. "And remember . . . if anyone calls—"

"I know, I know," Lila shrieked. "You're in the tub. Have fun. I'll be waiting up to hear all about it."

Jessica took a deep breath. From now on, she reminded herself, I'm not twelve years old. I'm fourteen and a half, and I'm a freshman at Sweet Valley High. She hurried outside to meet Josh, still barely believing that any of this was really happening.

"Hi!" Josh said in a low, warm voice. He gave a long whistle when he saw what she was wearing. "You look great. Even better than on roller skates."

"Thanks," Jessica said. She was thinking that Josh looked pretty good, too. He was wearing cotton chino pants and an off-white cotton sweater that showed off his tan. For a minute she felt fear wash over her. Would she really be able to pull this off? But then Josh went around to open the car door for her, and she felt that everything was going to be all right. All she had to do was act natural—and just remember that she wasn't twelve anymore!

"I thought your idea about a movie was great," Josh told her, starting the car. "You don't mind if my friend Sam and his girlfriend join us, do you? I told them we'd pick them up and grab a quick bite to eat first."

"That sounds fine," Jessica said. Actually she would much rather have Josh all to herself. "What's Sam like?"

"He's on the soccer team with me. He's nice—kind of quiet, but nice." Josh steered the car expertly down the tree-lined street. "And Melanie, his girlfriend, is a wonderful girl. She's a freshman, too. Maybe you two know each other."

Jessica felt her heart sink. That was all she needed. How was she ever going to be able to claim she was a freshman now? Wouldn't Melanie know she was lying right away?

"What's her last name? I can't think of anyone named Melanie," she said, trying to sound calm.

"Northrop. She's really cute. About your height, with blond hair cut like this—" Josh made a motion with one hand to indicate a pageboy. "She's super involved in school activities. She's on the j.v. cheering squad, she's secretary of the Student Council, and she sings in the glee club. I'm sure you'll recognize her."

Jessica slumped down in the seat. She was sure she *wouldn't*. She could already tell Melanie was going to see right through her in one second flat. This was clearly going to call for quick thinking.

First they picked up Sam. Sam Morse was a little shorter than Josh, and stockier. He *did* seem a little quiet, but he had a nice smile. "What's the plan for tonight?" he asked as they headed over to Melanie's house.

"Well, we thought we'd get something to eat and then see a movie," Josh said. "What do you feel like?"

"I'm broke," Sam admitted. "My dad cut my allowance this week, and Melanie's broke, too. Can we make it someplace really inexpensive for dinner?"

"How about the Dairi Burger?" Josh suggested.

Jessica felt her heart sink again. The Dairi Burger was a hamburger joint downtown—a popular spot with the high school crowd. Even the Unicorns went there all the time. In fact, Jessica had an uneasy feeling that some of them might be there tonight. And she was too dressed up for it.

"How does that sound to you, Jessica?" Josh asked politely.

"Oh, it sounds fine," Jessica lied bravely.

Josh patted her hand. "You're a good sport," he said, giving her a special smile. Jessica felt her spirits lift immediately. Maybe this wouldn't be so bad, after all. If she ran into anyone she knew from school, she'd just pretend she didn't recognize them.

They had stopped now at a small, Spanish-style house on the other side of town. Sam got out of the car to get Melanie, leaving Josh and Jessica alone.

"I still can't get over how pretty you look tonight," Josh said.

Jessica cleared her throat. She wished her voice were not quite so high. She sounded so *young*. "I'm really glad we met," she told him, letting her fingers rest lightly on the stick shift between them.

Sam opened the car door then, and Melanie—who fit Josh's description perfectly—jumped into the backseat. Like the others, she was wearing casual clothes. Jessica stuck out like a sore thumb.

"Hi, I'm Melanie," she said cheerfully, putting her hand out to shake. Jessica took it uncertainly. Whoever heard of shaking hands when you met someone? "Sam says you're a freshman at Sweet Valley High, too. Are you in Dawson's homeroom or MacPherson's? Are you taking college-prep bio or regular?"

Jessica swallowed.

"Hey," Josh said with a smile. "Don't barrage her with questions before we've even pulled away from the curb. Melanie, how does a hamburger and a movie sound to you?"

"It sounds fine." Melanie leaned forward so she could continue to quiz Jessica. "I can't believe we've never met," she said, her blue eyes fixed on Jessica's face with great interest. "What did you say your last name is?"

"Wakefield," Jessica said miserably, waiting for the inevitable look of recognition on the blond girl's face.

"I know Steven Wakefield. He's on the j.v. basketball team," Melanie said. "Are you related?"

"No," Jessica said. There was a brief silence and she added, "It's a common name, though."

Melanie looked at her closely. "Did you try out for the cheerleading squad? You look familiar to me, but I'm not sure why."

Jessica shook her head. "I haven't lived here long," she fibbed. "My family just moved to Sweet Valley from Chicago a few months ago. So I'm still kind of new around here and haven't met very many people yet."

Melanie instantly looked sympathetic. "Poor thing. It's really hard moving to a new place." Within seconds she was describing her own experience of moving when *she* was in the middle of sixth grade.

Jessica listened uneasily. She couldn't imagine anything ever being hard for Melanie. The girl seemed to have an answer to everything.

This whole thing wasn't going exactly the way she'd planned. She didn't know which she was more worried about—running into people she knew at the Dairi Burger, or having to endure more questions from Melanie.

Both seemed bad. But Josh had pulled up at the Dairi Burger now, and Jessica had no choice but to get out and try to seem as relaxed and mature as she could.

Something told her this was going to be harder than she thought. But it was too late to turn back now!

# Three

◇

"Well, you sure can't say this place has atmosphere," Sam said with a laugh. The four of them were sitting in a booth in the corner of the Dairi Burger, menus in front of them. Jessica didn't have much of an appetite. She was much too nervous that someone from school would come in and spot her.

"I love this place," Melanie protested. "It's got tons of atmosphere! Look, people have carved their initials in the wall. Sam, why don't you carve ours?"

Jessica looked at the wall next to her. Sure enough, the wood paneling was filled with tiny engraved messages. Josh turned red when Melanie mentioned the graffiti, and just then Jessica's eye fell on a heart near her elbow. Inside the heart were the words "Anita and Josh." She looked curiously at Josh. Could it be he? Who was Anita?

"Now," Melanie said, once they had all ordered hamburgers and cokes, "tell us about yourself, Jessica. I want to hear all about Chicago. Was it weird moving from a big city to a sleepy little town like Sweet Valley?"

Jessica thought fast. "No. I like Sweet Valley. The climate sure beats Chicago. And the people out West are so friendly." *And they sure ask a lot of questions*, she thought. She wished Melanie would just talk to Sam and leave her and Josh to talk about something else.

"Hey, wasn't that pep rally on Thursday afternoon a joke?" Melanie asked them all, unwrapping her straw when the waitress brought the sodas. "I couldn't believe all that fuss just for a soccer game." She winked knowingly at Jessica, who didn't have the faintest idea what she was talking about. "You'd think soccer was as big a sport as football!"

"I thought the rally was great," Sam protested.

"So did I," Josh said. "Soccer needs a lot more press. Boy, we usually have to wait till the last two minutes of a rally to even get announced."

Everyone looked expectantly at Jessica, who made a big production out of unwrapping her straw.

"I thought the cheerleaders looked rotten, though," Melanie said. "I mean, the j.v. squad has its problems, too—I'm not saying we don't. But did you see the way they collapsed when they tried to do that pyramid?"

"They did?" Jessica asked. She was on the booster squad, so she knew pyramids weren't all that easy to keep stable.

"Weren't you there?" Melanie demanded.

"Uh, I was sick on Thursday," Jessica said weakly.

"Hey," Melanie said, frowning in the direction of the door. "Do you know those girls over there, Sam? I think the redhead is Anita Pearce's sister. But why are they pointing at us?"

Jessica turned to follow her gaze. Her heart sank as she saw the knot of sixth graders coming through the door. Caroline Pearce, the biggest gossip in the whole middle school, was right in front, pointing at Jessica and snickering. Jessica felt her face turn flaming red—as red as Caroline's hair. Behind Caroline were Cammi Adams, Melissa McCormick, and Kerry Glenn. They weren't Jessica's friends, but she knew them—and they knew her. What if they tried to come over and start a conversation?

"What's wrong?" Josh demanded as Jessica squirmed closer to the wall, twisting her head to make herself as invisible as possible. "You look as if you just sat on a nail."

*So much for being elegant and sophisticated*, Jessica thought, squirming even farther away from him. *He must think I'm incredibly weird.*

"Jessica, do you know those girls? They seem to be looking at you and making the strangest faces," Melanie said. The waitress brought the hamburgers, and Jessica dove for hers with immense relief.

"This hamburger looks great," she said. "I'm starving."

Caroline and the rest of the girls walked right past their booth on the way to their own table, and Caroline hesitated. "Hi, Melanie. Hi, Jessica," she said loudly.

Jessica took a bite of her hamburger and stared straight in front of her. Make her go away, she thought. Don't let her stand there humiliating me.

"Jessica," Melanie said. "Your friend is trying to talk to you!"

By now Caroline, feeling snubbed, had moved on. "I don't think she meant me," Jessica said, putting down her hamburger. "Maybe there's someone else here named Jessica. I vaguely recognize her, but I don't know why she'd be talking to me."

Melanie stared at her, but luckily Josh decided to change the subject. "Let's figure out what movie we should see," he said, picking up the newspaper he had brought along. "What do you guys feel like? Something scary or something funny?"

"Hey," Sam said, his mouth full, "I've been dying to see that new horror movie *Night Stalker*. It's supposed to be awesome."

Melanie pretended to be upset. "We don't want to see something scary. Let's go see that new French film at the Apollo—*Marie Jean*. It's supposed to have a great love scene in it."

"That's rated R. Don't you have to be seventeen?" Jessica blurted out.

"So what? That's what a fake ID is for," Sam and Melanie said at the same time.

Jessica turned red. "Didn't you tell them I'm not even sixteen? I don't have a fake ID card," she said to Josh.

Josh looked embarrassed. "Jessica's only—" He paused. "Only fifteen," he said. "Let's go see *Night Stalker* instead."

"That's rated R, too," Sam said mournfully. "Besides, Melanie's the same age as Jessica and we see R rated movies all the time."

Jessica stared down at her plate, feeling awful. It was obvious that she was keeping them from having any fun at all. If she weren't here, they could go see anything they wanted. Now they were going to be stuck watching *Bambi* or something.

She was so mortified by the time they left the restaurant that she barely cared anymore. She didn't even notice when Caroline Pearce waved wildly at her.

What a disaster, she thought sadly. Her first real date, and she was striking out. It was bad enough that Josh thought she was a total deadbeat because she didn't seem to belong to anything at school—or even know what was going on. Now it looked as though she wasn't any fun outside of school, either!

But her spirits lifted a little when they got to the movie theater. It was fun being part of a foursome, looking so grown-up. Now that they were safely out of the Dairi Burger, she began to relax a little. When

Sam and Josh left to get popcorn, she actually began to enjoy Melanie's chattering.

"So tell me how you and Josh met," Melanie urged. "The last I knew, he'd had a big fight with Anita and Anita was heartbroken."

Jessica tried to look knowing. "Oh, that's all over," she said confidently. "You know how it is." *Who is Anita?* she was thinking to herself.

"Yeah, I know all about it." Melanie sighed dramatically. "You don't have to tell me. It took Sam *six whole months* to get over Laurie Beth, his old girlfriend. Anyway, I think you two make a cute couple," she added.

Jessica tried to sit up straighter. Now that they were sitting down in the movie theater she realized how tired she was. Acting fourteen and a half was much harder work than she'd expected.

But when Josh and Sam came back it was a little easier. They alternated seats, boy-girl-boy-girl, and Josh put his arm around her as soon as the lights dimmed. Jessica could barely concentrate on the movie, which was a silly comedy about a bunch of kids at summer camp. Josh's arm felt warm and strong around her. She inched a little closer to him and he squeezed her shoulder. "You're a sweet kid," he whispered.

Jessica drew back. *"Sweet kid"? In Elizabeth's sophisticated blue dress?* She didn't like the sound of that. Josh acted as if she were about ten. Jessica's lower lip stuck out as she watched the rest of the movie. She was so busy thinking of ways to prove to

Josh that she was every bit as grown up as he was that when the lights came on she was astonished.

"That," Melanie said, "was absolutely darling! Don't you think Robbie Robins is a total doll?"

She aimed her question straight at Jessica, who didn't have the faintest idea which one was Robbie Robins. "Yeah, he's OK," she said.

She didn't blame Melanie for looking disappointed. Who wouldn't be disappointed, trying to carry on a conversation with someone who lacked total enthusiasm.

What amazed Jessica was that Josh didn't seem to have noticed what lousy company she'd been all night. After they dropped off Sam and Melanie, he drove her back to Lila's house. It was eleven-thirty.

"Tonight was fun," he said, looking at her. "What do you have planned for next weekend? Do you want to go out again?"

Jessica was shocked. She had been convinced he'd never want to see her again after tonight. "That would be nice," she managed.

"Hey," Josh said suddenly, snapping his fingers. "I know what we can do! I've got a great surprise. Can you go out on Saturday night?"

"Uh, sure," Jessica said. What on earth was she going to tell her parents? Well, she would have to think of something. She wasn't going to turn down a second date with a guy as wonderful as Josh Angler.

"I'll call you in the middle of the week to make definite plans, but let's make it Saturday for sure,"

Josh said. He leaned over then and cupped her chin in his hand. "I mean it. You're a sweet kid," he said. And he kissed her on the lips, very, very gently. Jessica could hardly wait to get inside and tell Lila all about it.

"Jessica!" Lila cried, opening the door to her bedroom and padding out into the hallway in her flowered nightgown. "How was it? Did you have fun? What time is it?" She rubbed her eyes sleepily. "It feels like it's the middle of the night."

"Oh," Jessica said casually, "I don't know. It's early—not even midnight yet."

"Tell me everything," Lila insisted as they walked back into her room. "I want to hear every single word. Did he like your dress? Did you guys go somewhere really romantic?"

Jessica tried to look as mysterious as possible. "Lila," she said condescendingly, "you don't *need* a romantic setting to be romantic."

"Where did he take you for dinner? Someplace really fancy with lots of crystal and candles and everything?" Lila asked.

Jessica kicked off her sandals and plopped down on the bed next to Lila. "As a matter of fact, we just went to a quiet neighborhood place," she said. She didn't feel like saying *which* quiet neighborhood place. "But it was really special. And then we went to see a movie. Josh had his arm around me the whole time," she added.

Lila's eyes widened. "You're kidding! Were you two alone?"

"No, we were with some friends of his. You know how it is," Jessica added imperiously. "Older guys like to be more laid back about dating. They usually like to get together in a group."

"How do you know?" Lila asked suspiciously. "Jessica, this is the first older guy you've ever gone out with. You don't know any more than I do about what they like to do."

Jessica refused to let this squelch her. "After the movie came the best part of all. When he drove me back here he started to talk about what a great time he'd had . . . and then—oh, you don't want to hear about it," she said with a torturously dreamy look on her face. She waved her hand. "Let's just go to bed. I'm pooped."

"Jessica!" Lila screeched. She clapped her hand over her mouth. "Oooopps—I'll wake Mrs. Pervis. You're not going to bed until I hear every single detail."

Jessica giggled and let herself be yanked back down to a sitting position. "Well, he kissed me. And, Lila, it was absolutely wonderful. I think I'm in love!"

Lila's eyes were as big as saucers now. "He really kissed you? You mean right on the lips, not just on the cheek?"

"Right on the lips," Jessica said triumphantly. "And he wants to go out with me again, too. Next Saturday."

Lila stared. "But—what are you going to tell your parents? Are they going to let you go out with somebody who's older than Steven?"

"Of course not!" Jessica looked at Lila as if she were out of her mind. "They'd kill me if they knew I'd gone out with Josh tonight. No, I'll have to make up some kind of excuse for where I'll be." She gave Lila a significant look. "Your dad's out of town for a few more weeks, right?"

"You're welcome to stay here," Lila said. "He doesn't get back till a week from Tuesday, and Mrs. Pervis doesn't care. But won't your parents wonder why you're sleeping over so much?"

Jessica nodded. "You're right. I guess the thing to do is to stay here but tell my parents I'm staying somewhere else." She yawned. "I'm too tired to think about it now. But I know I can think of something."

Lila looked at Jessica with admiration. "I can't even believe you," she said. "Going out with a sixteen-year-old! It's absolutely amazing."

Jessica didn't answer. The truth was, she was tempted to agree.

# Four

◇

It was Tuesday afternoon and Elizabeth and her best friend, Amy Sutton, had just been dropped off by Amy's mother at the Valley Mall. She had promised to pick them up in an hour, when she was done shopping, so the girls had plenty of time to look around.

"Let's go to the Book Nook," Elizabeth suggested. "I want to see if anything new has come in." Elizabeth loved reading. It was one of the endless sources of disagreement between her and Jessica. Jessica thought books were dull. She would much rather be outside at the beach or talking on the telephone than curled up somewhere with a book.

But Amy liked to read almost as much as Elizabeth, and she loved the bookstore. Soon the two girls were happily immersed in the new paperback shelf in the young adult section. Elizabeth was so absorbed in reading the flap copy of a book by one of her favorite authors that she didn't notice when a tall, good-looking blond boy strolled up beside her and gave her a big smile.

"Hey," he said in a low voice, looking at her, "fancy running into *you* here!"

Elizabeth jumped. "Huh? Wh-what do you mean?" she stammered.

The boy kept smiling at her. "What are you looking at?" he asked her.

Elizabeth showed him the book. He was incredibly cute, whoever he was. She couldn't help feeling a tiny bit flattered. He looked old—even older than Steven. It wasn't every day that a cute older guy started a conversation with her!

"Hmmmm," he said, handing her back the book. "Looks like *girls'* stuff." He gave her a wink. "I like sci-fi better myself."

"Oh," Elizabeth said, feeling stupid. She looked at him more closely. He had nice warm brown eyes and wonderful, wavy blond hair, and she thought his smile was pretty charming. Usually Elizabeth didn't notice guys that much. In fact, it drove her crazy when her twin went on and on about various rock stars, but she had to admit that this guy was special.

"Well, I've got to get going," the boy said. He leaned over, pretending to look at a book next to Elizabeth. "I'm assuming you don't want your friend to know that you know me," he whispered, right against her ear. "But don't forget about Saturday night. I've got a great surprise for you." And with that he backed up, smiling, until he turned and strolled away.

"Wow," Amy said, wide-eyed. "Liz, do you know who that is? It's Josh Angler. Caroline Pearce pointed him out to me once. I think he's a friend of her sisters. He goes to Sweet Valley High. He's really popular—he's on the soccer team and everything. Do you think he likes you?"

Elizabeth frowned. "No. I think he thought I was someone else," she said suspiciously.

"You mean . . ." Amy stared at her. "You don't mean Jessica, do you?"

Elizabeth nodded. "That's the only thing that makes sense. People always get us confused— especially people who don't know us that well. That guy—Josh—obviously thought he knew me. Since I've never seen him before in my whole life, he must have met Jessica somewhere."

Elizabeth repeated what Josh had whispered to her, and Amy's blue eyes got even wider. "Wow," she said. "Do you think Josh and Jessica . . . I mean—"

"I don't know what kind of jam Jessica's gotten herself into now," Elizabeth said. "But from what that guy whispered to me, it's obvious that they're supposed to meet."

"Lizzie! What are you going to do?" Amy demanded. "She can't go out with Josh Angler. He's much too old for her!"

Elizabeth didn't say anything. She set the book she'd been looking at back on the shelf. "Come on," she said to her friend. "Let's get out of here. I need to sit down and figure out what to say to Jessica to keep her from doing something crazy."

Elizabeth was sitting on the lowest branch of the big pine tree in the Wakefields' yard. It was her favorite place to be when she wanted to be alone—especially when she had a problem to mull over as she did now.

It didn't take her long to guess what must have happened. After all, Jessica had been going on and on for weeks about older guys. Somehow she met this guy, and one thing led to another, and they'd made plans to get together on Saturday night. Elizabeth knew Jessica had a tendency to be impulsive and to do exactly what she pleased, but this time her sister was really going too far. First of all, there was no getting around the fact that their parents would *kill* Jessica if they knew. Going out with an older boy without permission was bad enough. And sneaking around would make it a cardinal sin! Elizabeth still remembered the trouble that had arisen when—months ago—Jessica sneaked out to the big Johnny Buck concert without her parents knowing. And this time—with a *boy* involved—it could be even worse!

But Elizabeth's concern for Jessica went deeper. Usually there was a good reason for the rules her parents set up, and she sensed that this time the reason was simple. Going out with an older guy was a situation the twins were simply too young to handle. Who could tell what kind of trouble Jessica could get herself into?

"I'm going to have to do something to stop her," Elizabeth declared. She jumped up off her "thinking seat" and hurried into the house. Jessica, as it turned out, was just turning her bicycle into the driveway, her blond hair streaming out behind her.

"Lizzie!" Jessica crowed, jumping nimbly off the bike and wheeling it into the garage to park it against the wall. "I'm so glad you're home! Will you help me make dinner tonight? I absolutely *promised* Lila I'd call her the second I got back, only I ran into Ellen and some other kids and now I'm late, and—"

Elizabeth looked stern. She had bailed her twin out of her chores too often that week already. "Lila can wait," she said. "I'll help you, but that means *help*—not replace! So you have to stick around." Ordinarily Elizabeth wouldn't have been so generous, but she thought this would be a good chance to ask Jessica some questions.

Jessica looked unhappily at the defrosted hamburger meat Mrs. Wakefield had left out for them. Now that their mother worked part time, the twins often helped prepare dinner. Jessica thought it was a crime. "I really need to call Lila," she grumbled.

"Never mind. She'll still be there when you're finished here," Elizabeth said sweetly, taking lettuce out of the refrigerator to start the salad. "You know," she said thoughtfully, "Amy's mom has been talking about taking a bunch of us to that new movie at the Valley Cinema. How would you like to get together a group and go see it?"

"Sounds fun," Jessica said, unwrapping the meat. "Except for the Amy Sutton part, that is." Jessica thought Amy Sutton was a big bore.

Elizabeth ignored this last comment. "Good," she said matter-of-factly, watching her twin closely out of the corner of her eye to see what her reaction would be to the rest of the proposed outing. "How about Saturday night? Amy says that's best for her."

Jessica's eyes widened. "Saturday? *This* Saturday night? I can't," she said abruptly. "I'm already doing something."

*Ah ha!* Elizabeth thought. "Oh, really?" she said nonchalantly, taking out oil and vinegar to make salad dressing. "What are you doing?"

Jessica thought fast. "Uh, I think I'm going to Kerry Glenn's cabin with her family. It's up near Tahoe. She's asked me a couple of times, and I've never been able to go before."

Elizabeth looked at her closely, wondering if she was telling the truth. She had to hand it to her twin. If she was fibbing, it sure didn't show!

"I didn't know you were going away," Elizabeth said. "Have you told Mom and Dad yet?"

"Nope. It's not definite. In fact, one of the things I have to do before dinner is call Kerry," Jessica said. "Lizzie, *please* finish up here for me. Just this once. I want to get everything straightened out so I can ask Mom and Dad tonight."

Elizabeth sighed. She hadn't really accomplished anything. She hadn't managed to warn Jessica off older guys, and now she was stuck making dinner! The memory of her strange run-in with Josh at the mall was fading, and Elizabeth found herself wondering if she hadn't overreacted a bit.

In all likelihood Jessica was telling the truth, and Josh had just mistaken her for someone else. Who could tell? Maybe she and Jessica had a look-alike somewhere that they knew nothing about!

"Lila," Jessica said into the phone. She had pulled the hall phone as far as she could into her bedroom and shut the door behind her, but even so she felt that she had to whisper for privacy's sake. With Steven and Elizabeth home, who could tell whether or not she was being overheard? "Listen, I have to figure out what I'm going to tell my parents about this weekend. It's still OK if I stay at your house, isn't it?"

"Sure," Lila said. Jessica could tell Lila was enjoying being involved in the drama. "Are you coming both Friday and Saturday nights?"

"Well, I kind of have to. I'm going to tell my parents that I'm going to Kerry Glenn's cabin for the weekend, so I'll have to pretend I'm away *somewhere*."

Lila thought this through. "Are you going to tell Kerry you're using her as a cover?"

"I don't see why I should. It'll just make everything much more complicated," Jessica said. "Besides, my parents never run into the Glenns. And Kerry doesn't come over here much. I can't possibly see how they could figure it out."

"Well," Lila said doubtfully, "I guess you're right. Do you know where you and Josh are going on Saturday?"

"No," Jessica said, "but he promised it would be somewhere really special. What do you think I should wear?"

"It depends what somewhere really special means." Lila giggled. "If it's like the last time, maybe you'd better try to wear something casual."

Jessica heard her father's tread on the stairs. "Uh, oh. My parents are home. I'd better get off the phone."

"Call me later," Lila said urgently. "I want to know exactly what you tell them!"

The Wakefields were having dinner when the phone rang. "I'll get it," Steven and Jessica said at once, both jumping up from their chairs.

"I'll get it," Mrs. Wakefield corrected them, reaching for the phone. "Yes, this is the Wakefield residence," she said into the phone after listening briefly. She turned to stare at Jessica. "She is. Can I tell her who's calling?"

Jessica squirmed in her seat.

"It's Josh," Mrs. Wakefield said, covering the phone with her hand. "Josh Angler. Would you mind if I asked him to call back after dinner, dear?"

No phone calls interrupting dinner was a household rule.

"Fine," Jessica murmured, staring down at her plate. She could feel her brother's and sister's watchful eyes on her.

"Who's Josh?" Steven demanded, taking a bite of his hamburger and eyeing his sister. "Don't tell me *boys* are starting to call my baby sister."

"I'm not a baby," Jessica said hotly.

"So who is he?" Steven went on, enjoying her discomfort. "You're bright red, Jess. You look even weirder than usual."

Jessica played with her salad, her lower lip sticking out. She hated it when Steven teased her. "Listen," she hissed, "I don't bug you when girls call you, do I?"

"Jessica's right," Mrs. Wakefield said with surprising firmness. "Her friends are her own business." She smiled at Jessica. "He sounds nice, dear. As long as he doesn't call during dinner, I don't see what right any of us have to bother you about it."

Elizabeth looked darkly at her sister. *She* saw a good reason to bother Jessica about it. What had happened at the mall could not have been an accident. How many guys named Josh could there be in a small town like Sweet Valley—and how many interested in Jessica Wakefield?

Jessica was fidgeting like mad. "I almost forgot," she said to her mother. "Kerry Glenn invited me to go with her family up to their cabin this weekend. It sounds great. It's right on a lake and everything. Can I go?"

Mrs. Wakefield raised her eyebrows, looking quizzically at Mr. Wakefield. "Well, we're going to need to know a little bit more about it, honey. Where is the cabin? Are the Glenns going to drive you? And, when are you planning on going and coming back?"

Jessica shrugged. "We haven't figured all that stuff out yet. I thought I'd ask first."

"Well, it sounds to me like I ought to call Mrs. Glenn," Mrs. Wakefield said slowly.

"No!" Jessica exclaimed. "I mean . . . her mom is out of town. I'll talk to Kerry and get all the information by tomorrow. I promise."

Mrs. Wakefield looked skeptical. "I'd feel better if I could talk to Mr. or Mrs. Glenn. Maybe later in the week. And meanwhile, find out everything you can about the trip and what you'll need to take with you."

Jessica nodded, forcing herself to eat a forkful of salad. It was funny how much more complicated it was to tell a lie than Jessica ever thought it would be. Now she was going to have to invent a reason why her mother couldn't talk to the Glenns.

But Josh had called her. And Saturday night would make all of this complicated scheming completely worthwhile!

# Five

◇

When Josh called back later that evening Elizabeth happened to answer the phone. "Jess!" she called, holding her hand over the receiver. "It's for you!"

Jessica picked up the phone in her bedroom and hollered—most inelegantly—that Elizabeth could hang up now. But Elizabeth paused, holding the receiver in her hand. She couldn't resist waiting just a minute to hear her sister get on the line.

"Jessica?" the low male voice inquired.

Elizabeth heard her sister giggle. "It's me, Josh," she said in a voice that Elizabeth could only think of as positively sickening. "How are you? I've been thinking about Saturday night," Jessica purred.

Elizabeth made a face. Yuck! She couldn't believe her sister was acting like such a jerk. She replaced the receiver gingerly, hoping Jessica was too engrossed to notice the little click.

"What's wrong, honey? You look as though you just ate something sour," Mrs. Wakefield commented from the couch, where she was reading the newspaper.

Elizabeth frowned. It was a real point of honor not to rat on her twin. She knew that her parents would have an absolute fit if they knew Jessica was sneaking around behind their backs, but she couldn't betray her sister. The thing to do was to confront her.

Elizabeth waited until Jessica was off the phone before storming upstairs. "Jessica," she said, putting her hands on her hips. "Who was that you were just talking to?"

Jessica's eyes were wide with innocence. "Lizzie," she said reproachfully, "I don't ask you who you were talking to when you've been on the phone. Don't you think we need to have a little privacy?"

Elizabeth sat down on the edge of her sister's bed, which was covered with clothes. "Hey!" she said, her expression darkening as she spotted a familiar-looking dress sticking out from under a heap of balled-up sweaters. "Isn't that my dress?"

Jessica stared down at the incriminating garment. "Uh, no," she said hastily, pushing a bunch of clothes on top of it. "It's just some old rag of Lila's that I borrowed."

"It is not!" Elizabeth cried, leaning over and

yanking the dress out. Wrinkled as it was, it was definitely her dress. "Would you mind telling me what it's doing in here—in this condition?" Elizabeth demanded.

Jessica had to come up with an explanation fast. The truth was, she had intended to wash and iron the dress and slip it back into her sister's closet. But she'd completely forgotten. She had to admit it looked pretty bad. "I . . . uh, I was just trying it on. I thought you wouldn't mind," she said desperately.

Elizabeth glared at her. "Since when do you just try on things of mine? And then leave them here in a heap?"

Jessica looked at her sister imploringly. "Please don't be mad at me, Lizzie. You know I go nuts when you yell at me. I know it was wrong to try it on; but . . . I like your taste so much, and—"

Elizabeth put her hands over her ears. "Stop," she groaned. "It's even worse when you try to butter me up. OK, Jess. I'll forget about the dress for now, as long as you wash it and iron it and get it back in my closet by tomorrow afternoon."

Jessica's eyes sparkled. Elizabeth could never stay mad at her for long.

"Anyway," Elizabeth said firmly, "there's something much more important on my mind. I want to know what you're doing talking on the phone to this guy Josh Angler? *And* I want to know what you're really planning to do on Saturday night."

The smile died on Jessica's face. "Wh-what are

you talking about?" she stammered. "Liz, I wasn't
. . . I'm not . . . who said anything about Saturday
night?"

"You did!" Elizabeth said. "I heard you. You
said, 'Josh, I've been thinking about Saturday night
all day.'"

Now it was Jessica's turn to be angry. "You were
listening in on me," she said accusingly.

Elizabeth reddened. "Only because I'm worried
about you, Jessica. You're not actually planning on
meeting this guy, are you? Amy told me he's in high
school. He's older than Steven!"

Jessica was quiet for a minute. "OK, Liz," she
said, relenting. "I'll tell you the truth, but only if you
swear not to tattle."

"I swear," Elizabeth said, her eyes big.

"I *did* meet an older guy. But I'm not going to
meet him on Saturday night. We just talk on the
phone, that's all. He's got the phone number of
Kerry's cabin, and he's going to call me there."

Elizabeth looked at her incredulously. "Wait a
minute," she said. "You really expect me to believe
that all you're going to do is talk to him on the
phone?"

"Well, believe what you want," Jessica said. "But
the truth is, that's all there is to it. Josh *is* too old for
me. I know that. I'd never do anything stupid like go
*out* with him. He's just fun to talk to, that's all."

Elizabeth began to feel foolish. "Where did you
meet him?" she asked uncertainly. She wondered if
she really had been making a big deal out of nothing.

"At the roller-skating rink with Lila last week. Ask Lila if you don't believe me," Jessica said. She tried to sound hurt, so Elizabeth would feel rotten for not trusting her.

Elizabeth was quiet for a minute. "I guess I owe you an apology," she said slowly. "I really jumped to conclusions. So you're actually planning on going to Kerry's cabin this weekend? You're not going to sneak out and see Josh?"

"Lizzie!" Jessica exclaimed innocently. "How on earth would I manage that?" She shook her head, her blond hair flying. "Honestly, Liz. You really ought to trust me a little more. And I don't want to keep saying it, but it really makes me feel bad that you felt that you had to listen in on my phone call." Her blue-green eyes were big and filled with hurt. "You could have just asked me."

Elizabeth truly felt awful now. "You're right, Jessie. I'm a jerk," she said. In a rush of guilt she scooped up the wrinkled dress. "To make up for it, I'll wash this myself," she said impulsively.

Jessica shrugged. "OK," she said. "If it makes you feel better, I guess I don't mind."

She waited until Elizabeth was out of the room before she breathed a sigh of relief. This was getting hard. She was going to have to make extra sure now to be careful.

"OK," Lila said, taking a deep breath. It was Wednesday afternoon and Jessica was over at the Fowlers' big house, coaching Lila on how to make her voice sound older. "Tell me once more what I'm supposed to say."

"Tell her that you're Mrs. Glenn," Jessica instructed. "That you just want to ask her personally if it's OK if I come to the cabin this weekend. You know how mothers sound! You need to really lay it on thick. Say all sorts of stuff about bringing extra sweaters because it's cold up in the mountains."

"OK," Lila said. "I'm ready." She looked skeptical. "But do you really think your mother will believe that I'm Mrs. Glenn?"

"Why not? She hasn't spoken to her that many times," Jessica said. "Come on! You've got to do it right now before you lose your nerve." Jessica hurried into the Fowler's den and picked up the extension so she could hear every word of the conversation.

Lila grimaced. "Here goes nothing," she said. She dialed the Wakefields' number, and after three rings Mrs. Wakefield picked up the phone.

"Hello?" she said.

"Is this Alice Wakefield?" Lila asked in a high, squeaky voice. "This is Nellie Glenn, Kerry's mother, calling." Jessica grimaced. Lila sounded so weird! She couldn't believe her mother was going to fall for this.

"Oh—oh, yes," Mrs. Wakefield said. "Jessica told me you might call this afternoon. She mentioned something about this weekend. . . ."

"That's *just* why I'm calling," Lila said. Jessica thought her voice sounded more like an old woman's than like a young mother's, but Lila was clearly getting into her role now and there was no stopping her. "We've been encouraging Kerry to invite a friend all year," she said in a confidential tone. "You know what they're like at this age. Kerry tends to be shy, and especially with her older brother being so domineering—and always wanting to invite *his* friends . . ."

Jessica rolled her eyes. She wished Lila would hurry up and get to the point.

But Mrs. Wakefield didn't seem phased. "Oh, I know just what you're saying," she said warmly. "I have a fourteen-year-old son, and I can sympathize. You're very kind to invite Jessica," she added. "Is there anything special she should bring?"

"Sweaters," Lila said promptly.

"Sweaters?" Mrs. Wakefield said, slightly confused.

"You know how crisp the mountain air can be," Lila said briskly. "She should bring several warm sweaters and a good warm bathrobe. That's all."

"Uh, fine," Mrs. Wakefield said. "And you'll be driving up to the mountains Friday afternoon, is that right? And coming back down on Sunday?"

"Yes, that's exactly right," Lila said. Her voice was starting to wobble a little. "The girls will have a wonderful time, I assure you, Alice. Don't you worry about Jessica one little bit."

Mrs. Wakefield sounded amused. "I won't, Nellie," she said. "I'm sure Jessica will have a marvelous time. I just hope she isn't any trouble."

"Trouble? Jessica? Good heavens," Lila said. "Why, she's such a polite, such a sweet-tempered, such a—"

"Cut it out," Jessica hissed from the den, covering the extension with her hand so her mother wouldn't hear her. She really thought Lila was going too far now.

Lila covered the phone with her hand. "I'm doing the best I can," she snapped in a whisper. "Just give me a break."

"What was that?" Mrs. Wakefield asked, confused.

"I was just saying what delightful company your daughter is. And I'm looking forward to the weekend very much."

"Fine. She'll be all ready to go on Friday afternoon," Mrs. Wakefield said. "And thanks again!"

"There," Lila said, setting down the receiver. "Admit I did a good job."

"You think she believed you were Mrs. Glenn?" Jessica asked doubtfully, hanging up the extension and wandering back into the kitchen.

"Of course she did! I was wonderful," Lila said confidently.

Jessica wasn't so sure. She got her books together and stood up to leave. She wanted to get home as quickly as possible to see what her mother said.

"You just have to hope your mother doesn't run into Kerry Glenn or her family," Lila added. "That's the thing about lying, Jess. It's best to keep it simple.

You seem to be making things incredibly complicated."

"Hi, Mom!" Jessica called, coming in through the front door and dropping her books and jacket on the bench in the foyer.

"Hi, sweetheart. How was school?" Mrs. Wakefield asked. She was in the kitchen, making dinner.

"OK. Nothing special." Jessica helped herself to an apple from the fruit bowl. "I had lunch with Kerry," she said nonchalantly. "She said her mom was going to call this afternoon and give you all the details about this weekend."

"She called about half an hour ago," Mrs. Wakefield said. "She sounds kind of strange, honey. I hope you're going to remember to be nice and polite, even if Kerry's family proves to be on the eccentric side."

"I'll be nice, Mom. I promise," Jessica said. She polished the apple on her sweater, feeling an enormous sense of relief. Her mother had believed that Lila was Mrs. Glenn!

As far as she could see, everything was taken care of now. She had convinced Elizabeth that she and Josh weren't actually meeting. And now she had everything lined up for a weekend in the mountains. Her heartbeat began to quicken. She could barely wait for Saturday night.

She knew—she just knew—that it would be absolutely magical. However much trouble she'd gone to, it would be worth it!

# *Six*

◇

Everyone was in high spirits at the Wakefields' house on Wednesday evening. Steven was in a great mood because the j.v. basketball team had beaten Ridgedale High the night before, and he had scored a whopping twenty points. Elizabeth was in a good mood because she'd received special praise for the latest edition of *The Sweet Valley Sixers*, the middle school paper of which she was editor. And Jessica was so excited about Josh—and Saturday night—that she felt as if she were walking on air. The twins were helping Mrs. Wakefield take the lasagna out of the oven and finish setting the table when Mr. Wakefield burst through the door, waving a bunch of tickets.

"Guess what I got at work today!" he exclaimed,

without even saying hello. "Five tickets to the circus for Saturday night!"

Steven clapped his hand to his forehead. "Dad, I completely forgot. A friend of mine at school got extra tickets for me and two other friends. I promised I would go with them."

Mr. Wakefield looked briefly disappointed. "Oh, well," he said. "I was hoping we could go as a family, but as long as you'll get a chance to go . . . maybe we can all meet at intermission."

Jessica carried the steaming pan of lasagna over to the table, her face set. "You forgot about me, too," she said. "I'm going to be up in the mountains with Kerry's family. Remember?"

Mr. Wakefield took off his coat, frowning. "I guess my surprise isn't much of a surprise."

"I'm dying to go to the circus!" Jessica wailed. "I've gone every single year. I can't stand the thought of missing it."

"Well," Mrs. Wakefield said philosophically, "I suppose you could call Kerry and tell her what happened. I'm sure she'd understand. You could probably arrange to reschedule your trip to the Glenns' cabin for some other weekend."

Jessica thought this over. The truth was that she *really* wanted to go to the circus. For a brief moment she wondered whether it wouldn't be worth it to call Josh and cancel. Would it really be more fun going out with him—blue sports car and all—than going to the circus with her family? To be honest, their date had been kind of uncomfortable for Jessica. Pretending to be fourteen and a half had taken a lot out of her.

Jessica couldn't decide what to do. She wanted to go to the circus badly. But she'd promised Josh she'd go out with him, and she'd gone to so much trouble to arrange everything. "I guess I should go to Kerry's house," she said mournfully, "but it kills me, the thought of missing the circus while you guys are all there."

Mrs. Wakefield put her arm around her. "It's very admirable for you to stick to your plans, dear. Kerry would probably be very disappointed if you canceled. From the way her mother sounded, she's been looking forward to bringing a friend. I think you're doing the right thing."

Jessica stuck out her lower lip. "Still," she said sadly, "I wonder if they're going to have those three clowns on the unicycles like last year?"

Steven groaned. "Something tells me this is going to be the most agonizing decision of the year for you, Jess. Why don't you just go ahead and bag out of this cabin trip? It's obvious that you'd rather go to the circus."

"Let's eat, before the lasagna gets cold," Mrs. Wakefield said. "We can talk about this more at the dinner table."

"Yeah, let's eat," Steven said eagerly. The twins rolled their eyes. Steven's appetite was the brunt of many family jokes.

"Watching you eat dinner is a circus all in itself,"

Jessica muttered. "Who needs to feel bad about Saturday night when there's a private clown act right here in the kitchen?"

"Jessica," Mr. Wakefield said thoughtfully, unfolding his napkin. "It seems to me you're in a rotten situation and it's partly my fault. If I'd sent away for tickets on time we would have scheduled this as a family outing as we usually do. Then you would never have agreed to go away for the weekend. Unfortunately I was so busy at work that I forgot."

Jessica poked morosely at her lasagna. She didn't see how this was supposed to make her feel better about missing out on the circus.

"I think," Mr. Wakefield continued, looking at his wife with a smile, "that if your mother agrees, we ought to arrange a special excursion—just you and me—for *next* weekend. I know it won't be as good as the circus, but at least it might help . . . a little."

Jessica took a tiny bite of lasagna. "Well," she said slowly, "I guess that might be kind of fun. I mean, it won't be the circus, but it'll be fun to go somewhere . . . just us." Her face brightened considerably. "Can we go out on the glass-bottomed boat from San Miranda?" Jessica had been dying to go on the glass-bottomed boat trip for ages.

"I don't see why not," Mr. Wakefield said.

Elizabeth looked at her sister with disbelief. Only Jessica, she thought, could take a situation like this and turn it into such an incredible advantage for herself. After all, *Jessica* was the one who'd arranged to go away for the weekend. Now she was going to end up having the fun of a weekend in the mountains, and a special excursion on top of it all!

"That sounds fun," Jessica said, sounding considerably more cheerful. She was remembering how cute Josh was and how much fun it had been to drive around Sweet Valley in his blue sports car. Granted, it wasn't easy pretending to be so much older than she was, but this time she was sure she'd feel much more natural. And even if she did have to miss out on the circus, she could console herself with the prospect of the glass-bottomed boat trip.

Elizabeth, sitting across from her, watched her twin with amazement. She didn't know how Jessica did it. She managed to rearrange everything so it worked out absolutely perfectly for her!

Everyone seemed to be feeling bad for Jessica now—as if missing the circus were the biggest disaster in months. They'd probably all be extra nice to her for days, Elizabeth thought grumpily.

But then, it *was* a shame her sister would be missing the circus. Even the glass-bottomed boat trip wouldn't be as much fun. Elizabeth vowed to try to be nice to her twin as well—even though she suspected Jessica would land on her feet.

She always did!

That evening after the dinner dishes were done, Elizabeth walked over to Amy's house. They were studying together for a math quiz the next day. But studying at Amy's usually meant having a long talk first to catch up on any news they might have missed since school let out that afternoon.

Amy was watching music videos on TV when Elizabeth came in. "Hey," she said, switching off the set with her remote control when she saw her friend. "I tried calling you, but your line was busy."

"Jessica!" Elizabeth groaned. "That girl spends more time on the telephone than the rest of Sweet Valley put together."

Amy's eyes were very round. "Jessica," she said importantly, "is exactly what I wanted to talk to you about. You'll never believe in a million years what I found out today."

"What?" Elizabeth demanded, plopping down beside her on the couch.

"Caroline Pearce told me this incredible story about Jessica's friend, Josh. But wait, let me make sure no one's around." Amy had a nosy little brother. She had to be sure he was upstairs before continuing. Once she'd made sure the coast was clear, she came back, her eyes bright with excitement.

"Now, you know Caroline, first of all," she said.

Elizabeth nodded. Caroline Pearce had the reputation of being one of the biggest gossips at Sweet Valley Middle school. All you had to do was tell Caroline a secret, and the whole world would know it soon after.

"Well, apparently Caroline's older sister, Anita, used to go out with Josh. In fact, they just broke up about three weeks ago."

"You're kidding," Elizabeth said. "You mean the same Josh who's been calling Jessica?"

"Yep. Caroline had a bunch of pictures from her family's trip to Disneyland a month ago, and there was one of Josh and Anita. I recognized Josh right away from that day at the bookstore. Anyway, I found out all kinds of stuff about him. He's sixteen. Caroline says he's really nice and smart and lots of fun. She also says Anita is crazy about him."

"So why did they break up?" Elizabeth wondered.

"Well, they got in a stupid fight about something. Caroline isn't sure what. She says Anita is pretty heartbroken about it all and she wants to get back together with him, but I guess she feels like it's too late."

"Wow," Elizabeth said. "This all sounds like something on a soap opera."

"Wait," Amy said, her eyes shining. "It gets a lot better. Or a lot worse, depending on how you look at it."

"What do you mean?"

"Well, Caroline says that she was pretty sure Anita wanted to get back together with Josh until this week. I guess a girl she knows from school—someone named Melanie, I think—told her that Josh had met someone new. Someone"—Amy lowered her voice for emphasis—"named *Jessica*."

Elizabeth stared at her. "You're kidding," she said finally. She remembered the innocent look on her twin's face when she insisted that her relation-

ship with Josh consisted only of phone calls. "Wow,"
she said again. "Amy, why do I get the feeling that
my twin sister has been hiding something pretty
major from me?"

"I don't know," Amy said, shaking her head.
"But it sure sounds weird to me."

Elizabeth didn't say anything for a few minutes.
Then she took out her books. "Let's get to work," she
said quietly. "I don't feel like talking about this anymore. I want to wait and do all the talking with
Jessica the next chance I get."

She was thinking that this time Jessica wasn't
going to get away with lying to her. She was going to
find out exactly what was going on between her sister and Josh Angler.

Jessica spent Wednesday evening locked in her
bedroom with the latest issue of *Ingenue* magazine,
trying to get ideas on everything from how to wear
her hair to how to show your date you're having a
good time. One article looked particularly interest-
ing: "The Second Date—How to Hang on Once
You're Hooked." Jessica read with great interest how
important the second date was. The author of the
article kept stressing how important it was to make
your date laugh, relax, and have a good time.

"Sometimes it helps to break the ice between
dates number one and two with a few casual phone
calls," the author added. "Don't let him think you've
forgotten him between weekends! Call him up and
say 'hi.'"

"Good idea," Jessica muttered, dragging the hall phone into her room. She had already looked up Angler in the phone book and had learned Josh's number by heart.

"Is Josh there?" she asked nervously when a woman answered. She wished her voice didn't sound so young.

"Anita?" the woman asked.

*Anita? Who was Anita?* she asked herself, the name sounding vaguely familiar. "No. It's Jessica," she said quickly. She hoped the author of the article was right. So far this phone call wasn't one bit fun.

"Hi, Jess," Josh said a minute later. "Mom, I've got it," he added. "What's up?"

"I'm just calling to say hi," Jessica said, feeling idiotic.

"I looked for you in school today," Josh said. "Didn't you say you were in Spaulding's geometry class? I waited outside for you after the bell, but you weren't there."

Jessica swallowed. Why hadn't it occurred to her that he might look for her in school? "I . . . uh, I wasn't in school today. I had a cold, so I stayed home."

"Oh, that's too bad," Josh said, sounding concerned. "Are you feeling better? You're still up for Saturday night, aren't you?"

"Oh, yes!" Jessica said. "What are we going to do?" she added curiously.

"Oh, it's a surprise. But I know you'll like it,"

Josh said. "Do I get to come in and meet your parents this time?"

"Ummm, no. I mean, I'm staying at Lila's house again," Jessica said.

"Really? Do you usually spend so much time over at her house?"

"She gets very lonely," Jessica said, defending herself. "She doesn't have any brothers or sisters, and her father is away so much. I like to spend as much time there as I can."

"Well, that's really nice of you. But one of these days I probably should meet your parents. Won't they wonder about me?"

"No," Jessica assured him. "I mean, they trust me. They don't need to meet every guy I go out with." That sounded a little clumsy, but it was too late to take it back. Jessica had to admit that making conversation with Josh wasn't as easy as she thought it ought to be. Maybe she and Josh weren't fated for each other, after all.

"So where do we meet? In front of Lila's house again?" Josh said.

"That would be easiest," Jessica told him. "What sort of clothes should I wear for this surprise evening?"

"Oh," Josh said, "anything you want. It isn't anything fancy, but I think it'll be fun. Actually, I have to check out a couple of things first. Can I call you back tomorrow night and tell you what time I'll be coming by for you? I think my cousin may be coming with us, and one of her friends. I need to check and see what time I'm supposed to pick her up."

"Sure," Jessica said faintly. Great, she was thinking. Another double date. As far as she was concerned that meant double the effort! And double the risk of someone finding out she was only twelve years old.

She hoped the surprise would make up for having to double-date again. Jessica was beginning to wish she'd gone with the rest of the family to the circus, after all!

# *Seven*

◇

Elizabeth wasted no time. The minute she got back from Amy's house she ran straight upstairs and knocked on Jessica's bedroom door.

"Just a sec," Jessica said. A minute later she opened the door, and Elizabeth clapped her hand over her mouth.

"Jessica!" she shrieked. "What's that goop all over your face?"

"Mud mask," Jessica said. "It's supposed to clear your complexion. Lila uses it all the time."

Elizabeth walked into her twin's bedroom, closing the door firmly behind her. "It's hard to talk to you seriously when you've got brown stuff all over your face. But I'll try. Jessica, I want to know exactly what's going on between you and Josh Angler—

because Amy Sutton just told me some stuff that I can't even believe. For instance, according to some girl named Melanie, you and Josh have been going out."

Jessica stared. How on earth had *Melanie* gotten back to Amy Sutton? The world seemed awfully small all of a sudden. "That isn't true," she said nervously. "Lizzie, I told you—it's just been a couple of phone calls. That's all."

Elizabeth wasn't going to be duped this time. She folded her arms across her chest and glared at Jessica. As hard as it was to be mad at her twin with that ridiculous facial mask on, she had to make sure Jessica understood that she couldn't fib her way out of this one. "Don't even try," she said. "Melanie said she went out on a double date with you guys last Saturday night. In fact, Caroline claims she saw you in the Dairi Burger with Josh."

Jessica dropped her eyes. This was going to be tricky. Obviously denying that she'd been with him wasn't going to work. "Lizzie," she said imploringly, "what's the big deal? All we did was go to a movie together. He's really nice and polite and everything. I know if you met him you'd realize it's all completely aboveboard."

"Yeah? Then why don't Mom and Dad know anything about it?" Elizabeth demanded.

Jessica didn't have an answer. She fidgeted nervously, trying to think of some way out.

"I don't suppose the fact that he's sixteen—two

whole years older than Steve—has anything to do with it?"

Jessica bit her lip. Elizabeth had her backed into a corner. The only recourse was to play completely dumb. "What are you talking about—sixteen?" she demanded. "Josh isn't sixteen. He's fourteen, the same age as Steven. He told me so himself. I asked him the day after you told me he was older than Steven."

Elizabeth gave her twin a pitying look. "Jessie," she moaned, "don't you realize what's happened? He must have lied to you about his age so you'd go out with him!"

"I don't know what you're talking about," Jessica said defensively. "Josh Angler wouldn't lie. He's incredibly sweet. And I know for a fact that he's only a freshman. He's told me all about playing j.v. soccer and what classes he's taking and everything. Anyway, since when do you know so much about him? How do you know he isn't fourteen?"

"Look, Jess," Elizabeth said gravely, sitting down on the edge of the bed. "I'm really sorry to have to be the one to break this to you, but Josh has been lying. He isn't fourteen. He's a junior, not a freshman. Which means he's sixteen!"

"I don't know what you're talking about," Jessica repeated. *What an actress I am,* she thought admiringly. She really managed to sound just right—horrified and angry at the same time—as if her sister were breaking her heart by revealing something she hadn't known about Josh.

"Caroline Pearce told Amy the whole story. Apparently Josh used to go out with Anita, Caroline's older sister."

"You're kidding," Jessica said. This *was* an honest-to-goodness shock to her. "When did they break up?" She narrowed her eyes. "Anita's really pretty," she added. "I wonder who broke up with whom."

"Well, Caroline didn't say." Elizabeth giggled. "And knowing Caroline, that probably means she doesn't know. But I guess they went out for a long time. And they just broke up recently. They had some kind of huge fight a few weeks ago."

Jessica was quiet as she mulled this over. That made sense. She had met Josh the week before—that was after Anita.

"I'm sorry to have to break all this to you," Elizabeth continued, patting Jessica awkwardly on the shoulder. "I know it must be hard, finding out that he's been lying to you about his age. He really told you he was fourteen?"

Jessica nodded, her eyes big and sad. "He really did," she said mournfully. "He told me all this stuff about the freshman class. And it sounded so realistic! I recognized all these teachers' names and everything from Steven. Boy," she said, shaking her head, "I've been such a jerk, Liz. I never in a million years would have gone out with him if I thought he was that old."

Elizabeth kept patting her shoulder. "Poor Jes-

sie," she said. "Well, I guess now you'll tell him you
can't meet him again, right?"

"Absolutely! We didn't have plans to meet again
anyway, but if he ever suggests it, you can count on
the fact that I'll say no," Jessica promised solemnly.
"Wow! If he's really *sixteen*, he's four whole years
older than I am." She shuddered. "Way too old! And
besides," she added, "I just feel like I can't trust him
anymore. What kind of guy would purposely lie
about his age?"

"You're right," Elizabeth agreed. "I mean, I can
understand his motivation. He obviously likes you
and was afraid—and rightly so—that you wouldn't
agree to go out with him once you knew his real age.
But it's a rotten, rotten thing to do. He could have
really hurt you. If I were you, I'd tell him exactly
what you think of the way he's behaved!"

Jessica nodded solemnly. "I will, Lizzie. I can't
thank you enough for telling me what Amy told you
tonight. You're a wonderful sister!"

"Well," Elizabeth said, mollified, "I'm just trying
to watch out for you, Jess. After all, I am four minutes
older. I've got to take responsibility for you!"

Jessica nodded. She was congratulating herself
for the best amateur acting job she'd done in ages.
Elizabeth really believed that she was shocked and
upset about Josh—and that she'd never go out with
him again.

The truth was, Jessica was more determined
than ever to make Saturday night work out. Espe-

cially now that she realized she had fierce competition.

Anita Pearce, she thought musingly. She wondered how much Josh still cared for her.

Just then the telephone rang. The girls looked at each other. "I'll get it," Jessica said, running out to the hallway to pick up the phone.

It was Josh.

"He's on the phone," she whispered, covering the receiver with her hand. "Lizzie, let me talk to him in private, OK? I want to tell him off."

Elizabeth nodded. She could certainly understand why her sister wanted some privacy. If she were Jessica, she wouldn't let Josh off lightly!

"Hi!" Jessica said sweetly into the phone once her sister had gone downstairs. "Are we all set now for Saturday?"

"All set. I just called my cousin to see what time I'm supposed to get her. She's really sweet. I think you'll like her. Actually, maybe you two know each other. She's a sophomore. Her name is Megan Moore."

"Megan . . ." Jessica said, pretending to search her memory. "That sounds familiar. What does she look like?"

"Light brown hair. Blue eyes. She's cute. She plays the saxophone in the band."

"I don't think I know her," Jessica admitted. "I've probably seen her around school, though."

"Well, she's bringing someone . . . I can't remember his name. Stu or Stan someone, I think. She says he's really nice. So I'll get Megan first, then pick you up in front of Lila's. OK?"

"And you *still* won't tell me where we're going?" Jessica wheedled.

"Nope. It's a surprise. But I promise we're going to have a great time."

"OK!" Jessica said happily. She had barely replaced the receiver when Elizabeth came back upstairs.

"Did you tell him off?" she demanded.

Jessica nodded, round eyed. "You would have been really proud of me," she said seriously. "I told him that I was shocked and upset that he lied to me that way. And that I was old enough to be taken seriously and what he'd done could've gotten me in real trouble with my family. I told him that I don't want to talk to him on the phone anymore and he shouldn't call me on Saturday night at Kerry's house."

"You did the right thing, Jess," Elizabeth said solemnly. "I know it was hard. But I'm sure you'll be glad later on."

Jessica got up to examine herself in the mirror. "I think it's time to take this stuff off," she said, poking the facial mask with a tentative finger. "If my complexion isn't radiant and glowing by now, it never will be!"

She hurried off to the bathroom, convinced she had set her sister's heart at ease.

"Steven, are you sure there's no way you can

join us on Saturday night?" Mr. Wakefield asked. Steven was sitting in the family room with his parents, watching the end of a television movie. The twins had already gone to bed.

"I'd like to, Dad. But to tell you the truth, I've got a hot date." Steven's dark eyes twinkled. "I'm actually pretty excited about it. This girl's amazingly nice. I met her after practice a few weeks ago, and we've started hanging around together at lunch and stuff."

"Hmmmm," Mrs. Wakefield said, smiling at him. "Sounds promising. What's she like?"

"She's great! She's got blue eyes—sort of your color, Mom—and long brown hair. She's a great musician, and she's a really good athlete, too. She's been talking about getting together for a while, but somehow we've both been busy. Anyway, she got some extra tickets from a friend of hers. So we're going to double-date with her cousin and someone else. It should be really fun."

"It's a shame," Mr. Wakefield commented, "about Jessica. I really want to make it up to her somehow. You know how much she loves the circus!"

"Yeah," Steven said sympathetically. "I really feel bad for her. I think she's doing the right thing, though. I mean, she did promise Kerry she'd go to her cabin. Besides," he added, "she'll have fun at the lake. It's not as if she's got to go somewhere rotten or anything."

"True. And taking her out on the glass-bottomed boat will help make up for it," Mrs. Wakefield said.

"But it is too bad we can't all go as a family again this year. It's always been such a Wakefield tradition," Mr. Wakefield said with a sigh. "Listen, Steven, promise me that we can all get together at intermission. That way you can introduce your new friend to your mother and me."

"Yes, we'd really like to meet her," Mrs. Wakefield said. "She sounds like a nice girl."

Steven looked more than a little infatuated. It wasn't too often that he sounded so excited about a girl, and his parents were intrigued.

"What did you say her name was again?" Mrs. Wakefield asked curiously. "Have you told us, or am I getting absentminded in my old age?"

"I didn't tell you. Actually, she's got a beautiful name. It's Megan," Steven told them. "Megan Moore."

# *Eight*

◇

By seven o'clock on Saturday night Jessica was so excited her stomach was doing flip-flops. She was dressed and ready, waiting for Josh to pick her up at Lila's house.

"Where do you think he's going to take you?" Lila asked. She was sprawled on the couch, watching Jessica pace back and forth, periodically checking the front window to see if the blue sports car had turned into the drive.

"I don't know," Jessica admitted. "We're double-dating again, this time with a cousin of his named Megan."

"Maybe it'll be somewhere really great. Maybe he'll take you to a fancy French restaurant or out on one of those boats where you can eat dinner and go dancing."

"I doubt it," Jessica said. She couldn't help smiling at her friend's idea of a romantic date. Lila was so used to a high standard of living that a burger at a local restaurant would seem terribly disappointing! Whereas for Jessica, just going out with Josh, and getting to ride around with him in his blue sports car, was more than exciting enough.

"He's here!" Jessica exclaimed, spotting the car through the window. "OK, Li, wish me luck. I'll be home by midnight," she added, checking her appearance once more in the mirror.

Once again she had changed her clothes at Lila's. She was wearing a pair of tight designer jeans and a cotton turtleneck sweater, which she hoped looked glamorous and sophisticated. Long, dangling earrings completed the look—copied from the *Ingenue* magazine she had pored over and practically memorized.

"Have fun!" Lila called after her. She giggled. "Don't do anything I wouldn't do."

Jessica took a deep breath as Josh came up the Fowlers' front walk. One peep out the window proved that he looked even more wonderful than she'd remembered. His blond hair was combed neatly, and he was wearing pleated cotton pants and a freshly pressed white shirt with the sleeves rolled up. He was so tanned and healthy-looking! Jessica's heart was already beating a little faster, and when he opened the door and gave her that warm smile she positively melted.

"You look great," Josh said appreciatively. "Really great." He leaned over and kissed her on the cheek. "Come on. I want you to meet Megan."

Jessica followed him down the walk to the car. But Megan had already bounced out to say hello. She was a tall, strikingly pretty girl with long brown hair and eyes the color of the California sky. "Hi!" she exclaimed. "I'm Megan Moore, Josh's cousin." She gave Jessica a big smile that put her instantly at ease. "He's already told me all about you and all I can say is, I must be a dope for not having met you at school by this time. Anyway, that's my fault. I spend so much time at band practice that I forget to get out and meet people."

"I'm that way, too," Jessica said. She glanced sideways at Josh. She was afraid he was going to think she was a complete nerd for never having met anyone at Sweet Valley High.

"Well, what do you say, Megan? Should we head over and collect your date?" Josh asked, taking his car keys out of his pocket.

Jessica felt a sudden heady rush of excitement. She could hardly believe this was all happening. Here it was, Saturday night, and she was really standing here talking to these people. They accepted her. They thought she was old enough to go out with them. And Josh—handsome, polite Josh with this adorable sports car—was her date. It was really astonishing if you thought about it.

"Hey," she said, clambering into the car next to Josh while Megan got into the back, "where are we going tonight? Or is it still a surprise?"

"You'll have to guess," Josh teased her, putting the car into drive. "Tell me where to go now," he instructed his cousin.

"Go straight down this road," Megan said. "I'll tell you when to turn right. He doesn't live that far from here."

"What do you mean, guess?" Jessica demanded. "Give me a clue!"

Josh was clearly enjoying himself. "Should I give her a clue, Megan?" he asked.

Megan pretended to think it over. "*I'll* give you a clue," she told Jessica. "It's on the casual side. And you'll have to be ready to expect the unexpected. You'll have to be ready to clown around." She giggled, and so did Josh.

Jessica frowned. "I don't get it. Give me another clue," she urged.

"Turn right here," Megan instructed.

Josh turned. "Here's another clue. It takes place in three rings," he said.

Jessica narrowed her eyes. "Three rings?" she repeated blankly.

Josh laughed at the confused expression on her face. "It's the circus!" he cried. "We're going to see the circus!"

"And turn left at that stop sign," Megan instructed.

Jessica's mouth dropped open. "The—the circus?" she stammered.

Josh nodded. "Yeah. You're not disappointed are you? I've always loved the circus, and I was so glad when Megan told me she had these tickets." He leaned over to pat Jessica's hand. "We're going to have a blast."

Jessica swallowed. "Yeah," she said. "I'm sure we will."

She slumped down in her seat, her mouth as dry as cotton. This was like a bad dream. How on earth was she going to manage to hide from her parents and Elizabeth at the circus? They were bound to run into one another! And her parents were convinced she was safely up in the mountains with the Glenns. They were going to kill her.

"Go straight up this street," Megan said, leaning forward.

Jessica, still in a reverie, looked around her with surprise. It suddenly occurred to her that they were driving back the exact same route she had taken to get to Lila's. They were only two blocks away from her house.

"Keep going," Megan said. "Now take a left here. It's that house right in the middle of the street."

Jessica felt as if she were suffocating. She could barely believe it when Josh turned the blue sports car into her own driveway. "Wh-what are we doing here?" she squeaked.

Josh looked at her strangely. "We're picking up Megan's date," he said.

"Oh, no," Jessica moaned. "I mean, oh, isn't that nice." She couldn't believe this was happening to her. She just wanted to get out of the car and run and hide somewhere—anywhere—before the inevitable happened.

"I'll go get him. You two just stay right here and catch up," Megan said brightly. Before either of them could respond she was out of the car and halfway up the walk. Jessica squirmed miserably, trying to think of some reasonable excuse for hopping out of the car and racing away as far as possible.

"Jessica," Josh said, looking slightly uncomfortable, "there's something I have to talk to you about. Actually I really wanted to tell you this on the phone, but I felt like it would be easier in person. And I think we'll both relax and have a better time tonight if I can get this off my chest. I know I never mentioned this to you before, but before I met you I had a steady girlfriend named Anita. We went out for a long time—over a year. And then we split up about a month ago."

Jessica twisted her bracelet around and around on her wrist. She really didn't want to hear about Anita now. She just wanted to get out of the car before her brother came out of the house.

"Well, we started talking a lot again, just on the phone and all," Josh said. He sighed. "I guess the truth is that we still have strong feelings for each other. She knows that I'm taking you to the circus tonight. In fact, she's going to be there, too. But—" His voice broke off, and he looked positively miserable.

"You're still in love with her, aren't you," Jessica

said mournfully. It figured. First he told her that he just happened to be taking her to the one place in town where her entire family was going to be. Then he drove straight to her own house to pick up her older brother for a double date. And now he was telling her that he was still in love with his old girlfriend. This was *not* the way things were supposed to go according to *Ingenue* magazine.

"Listen, Jessica," Josh said seriously, looking straight at her, "I really like you a lot. You're one of the nicest girls I've met in ages. But the truth is that I still feel pretty devoted to Anita. I'm not sure what's going to happen between us, but I feel that it would be wrong to lead you on. I'm just not sure I'm ready to give up what she and I had together."

Jessica stuck her lower lip out. This was a nightmare—a complete and total nightmare. "Maybe I should just go back to Lila's," she said, looking uneasily at the closed front door of her house. "I mean, I wouldn't want to come between you and Anita."

Josh looked horrified. "Absolutely not! Jessica, I really like you. I want to be your friend. At least let me take you out tonight and let's have a really good time together. We're definitely going to be friends."

Jessica wasn't so sure of that. As far as she was concerned, she'd be lucky if she could get through the evening without being ostracized by her whole family. She couldn't help thinking the whole thing was Josh's fault. If she hadn't met him that day at the stupid roller-skating rink none of this would ever have happened. And now look at the fine mess she was in!

But Jessica couldn't worry anymore about Josh and Anita. The front door opened, and Steven came out behind Megan, his hair neatly combed and his face radiant. He was obviously looking forward to a wonderful evening with his new girlfriend.

He was almost inside the car before he saw Jessica and stopped dead in his tracks.

"Steven, this is my cousin, Josh—and his date, Jessica," Megan said in her cheerful voice. "You guys, this is Steven Wakefield." She glanced anxiously at their blank faces. "We're not interrupting anything, are we?"

"No," Jessica said rapidly.

"Wakefield?" Josh repeated blankly, staring at Jessica. "But . . . that's your name," he added.

Jessica felt her face turn bright red. "It's a really common name," she muttered, praying Steven wouldn't give her away.

Jessica couldn't bring herself to look her brother in the eye. She didn't know how she was going to be able to bear this.

"There are lots of Wakefields," Steven said vaguely, looking at her as if she were a total stranger. "Josh, you're a junior, right? I've seen you play soccer." He turned back to his sister, an expression of feigned curiosity on his face. "What about you, Jessica?" The way he said her name made Jessica cringe. She could tell her brother had decided to torture her. "Are you a junior, too?"

"No," Jessica said. She stared straight ahead of her while Josh started the car up again. She just wanted this whole miserable ordeal to be over.

"Are you a sophomore?" Steven continued in a friendly, reasonable tone.

"She's a freshman," Josh said. "Like you."

"Oh, she is?" Steven said. Jessica felt sick. She was the only one who knew that Steven's friendly voice was actually dripping with sarcasm. She felt tears prick behind her eyelids.

"Well, we'll have to talk later," Steven said, staring at her with a murderous look in his eyes. "After all, we have so much in common. We're in the same class, we have the same name—"

"Yeah," Jessica said. "I guess we do have something in common."

She gave him the most imploring look she could muster. She was going to have to do something to keep him from blowing her cover. The question was, what?

"Now, would you mind telling me what is going on here?" Steven demanded. Josh had dropped them off and gone to park the car, and Megan had run over to say hi to some of her friends.

"Steven, don't give me away. Please. I'll explain everything later. I'll do anything you want me to—I'll clean your room for you for the next month," Jessica said desperately.

Steven shook his head. "I've got to hand it to you, Jess. Just when I think I have you all figured out, you go and do something so stupid, so ridiculous, that I realize I've got to start from scratch."

Jessica's eyes filled with tears. "Don't tell on me," she begged. "Come on, Steven. I'll die if you do."

Steven looked closely at her, and suddenly his expression seemed to soften a little. "You look upset," he said. "Are you OK? How in the world did you get yourself into this mess?"

Jessica's eyes widened in horror. "Steven, there're Mom and Dad and Liz," she moaned. "I'm going to go hide in the ladies' room until they're inside. Will you tell the others where I am?"

She didn't even bother to wait for his response. She just fled.

All she could do was pray that he wouldn't disgrace her by telling them that she wasn't fourteen at all, that she was really just his twelve-year-old baby sister.

# Nine

◇

The circus was taking place at the Valley Coliseum, a big indoor arena about fifteen minutes from downtown Sweet Valley. Jessica had been here every year with her parents, and she didn't have to ask where the ladies' room was. She just ran as fast as she could, keeping her head down. She couldn't believe it. She just couldn't believe it. If it had been somebody else it might have even been funny . . . but as it was it was nothing but a disaster. Jessica moaned as the full extent of her predicament struck her. She was on a double date—with her brother! What was going to keep Steven from making her the laughingstock of the whole group by telling them who she was?

And even—by some miracle—if Steven managed to keep his mouth shut, what was going to prevent her parents from seeing her? The way her luck was going so far, Josh and Megan had probably managed—just as an extra-special surprise—to get tickets right next to the Wakefields. Jessica hurried into the ladies' room and breathed a sigh of relief. She was safe—at least for the moment. Her fingers trembling, she began to comb her hair. The thing to do was to stay calm no matter what. Maybe—just maybe—it would work out all right, *if* she could manage to get through the evening without bumping into her parents or Elizabeth, and *if* Steven stayed quiet. Her reverie was interrupted as the door to the ladies' room swung open and Anita Pearce and her best friend, Diane Brown, came hurrying in. Jessica only knew Diane by sight. But looking at Anita, a sudden thought came to her. Wasn't this the perfect way out of the whole terrible jam? If she could convince Anita to come over and talk to Josh, maybe they'd make up. And Jessica could sneak home during the intermission.

"Anita," she said, turning around from the sink, "do you remember me? I'm a friend of Caroline's. Jessica Wakefield."

Anita nodded. "Caroline told me about you," she said stiffly. Her eyes looked puffy, as though she'd been crying.

"Listen," Jessica said quickly, "I don't blame you for acting funny. That's because you know I'm here with Josh tonight. But listen, Anita, he still really loves you. He told me so on the way over here. I think if you come over and talk to him . . . if you try

. . . that you two can get back together. In fact, I'm sure of it."

Anita and Diane exchanged glances. "Josh told you that he still likes me?" Anita repeated slowly.

Jessica nodded. "He and I are just friends," she explained. Actually Jessica wasn't even sure they were *friends*. At least they wouldn't be once Steven was done ratting on her.

"I don't know," Anita said sorrowfully. "I miss Josh like mad. But we had a huge fight, and I'm not sure I can—" She broke off. "I'm not sure I have it in me to tell him I'm sorry."

"Come on, Anita," Diane urged her. "I don't want to see you mope around all night the way you have for the past couple of weeks." She gave Jessica a smile. "Thanks for telling us, Jessica. I'll do my best to push Anita into talking to Josh—at least at some point tonight."

Great, Jessica thought. By the time Anita decided she was ready to apologize, the circus would be almost over and the Wakefields would surely have spotted Jessica. Maybe the thing to do was just to disappear right now. Josh wouldn't miss her for at least another five or ten minutes. By then she could be safe in a taxicab heading home.

But she'd still look like a moron that way. If Anita came over and made up with Josh, then she'd have a chance to back out gracefully, even to look like the hero of the day. That was what she'd just have to hope for.

Jessica got back to her seat just as the lights were

dimming and the master of ceremonies was coming out into the center of the middle ring. A spotlight lit up a big circle around him. "Ladies and gentlemen!" he boomed. "Welcome to the tenth annual visit of our circus to Sweet Valley!"

Thunderous applause greeted his announcement.

"Where were you?" Josh asked, helping her take off her jacket and arrange it on the seat behind her. "I was getting worried."

"There was a long line," Jessica fibbed. She shot a nervous glance at her brother. To her amazement, Steven winked at her. What was that supposed to mean? Was he just trying to drag out her torture?

"Our first act, ladies and gentlemen, will be preceded by the three most terrific clowns this side of the Rockies." A drumroll followed this, and everyone cheered. "Let me introduce (drumroll) Lo— (drumroll) Mo— (drumroll) and Bo!" A door in the corner of the big domed arena opened and three short, fat clowns rode out on unicycles, furiously pumping their horns. The crowd exploded into laughter and applause.

Steven leaned over, clapping, and whispered to Jessica, "Don't look now, but Mom and Dad are right across from us on the other side."

Jessica felt her face get hot. "Where?" she hissed.

"Right across from us. See? Liz is wearing that aqua shirt of hers. See them?"

Jessica nodded numbly. "Yeah," she said sorrowfully. "I see them."

"Just act normal," Steven whispered. "You look as if someone just told you there's a bomb threat."

"Aren't you going to tell on me?" Jessica whispered back.

"Is anything wrong?" Josh asked, looking at her worriedly. He had obviously heard them whispering and wanted to know what was going on.

"Nothing," Jessica and Steven said in unison, both sitting up straight and leaning away from each other. Jessica tried to keep her eye on the clowns' antics as the shortest rode in a small circle and the other two orbited around him. Usually she loved these clowns. But now all she could concentrate on was the spot across from the center ring where her family was sitting. Wouldn't they look around for Steven? She knew they'd spend ages trying to locate him in the crowds. And as soon as they did, she was done for.

The first act passed in a blur. A trapeze artist, a lion tamer, a special clown act, a fire-eater, and three dancing bears completed the first part of the evening. Everyone around her was having a wonderful time, but Jessica was fidgeting like mad. She kept trying different positions, hoping to obscure her face in case her parents looked her way. She had almost completely forgotten that she was supposed to be enjoying herself with Josh. She'd barely even said a word to him.

"Having fun?" Josh asked her when the finale of the first act—ballet dancers balancing on horseback—was completed.

Jessica stared nervously across the arena at her parents. The lights had come back on now, and people were getting out of their seats to stretch their legs or walk to the concession stand. The master of ceremonies announced that there would be a twenty-minute intermission.

And the Wakefields were getting out of their seats. Were they looking across at Steven and her? Had they spotted them? Jessica couldn't tell.

Just then a female voice greeted Josh. It was Anita, looking slightly sheepish. "Hi, you guys," she said, sitting down in an empty seat behind them. "I just thought I'd come over here for a few minutes and see how you're doing. Diane is buying popcorn."

Josh reddened, looking from Anita to Jessica. "Do you guys know each other?" he asked.

Jessica and Anita nodded.

"How are things?" Josh asked Anita. From the look on his face it was obvious how glad he was to see her. Jessica had a sudden wild hope that it wasn't too late yet for them to make up and give her a chance to escape without looking foolish—before her parents came over and caught her.

"This is pretty good, isn't it?" Anita asked, referring to the circus.

Josh nodded. "Not as good as last year, though." Apparently this had some kind of private meaning, because Anita blushed, and so did Josh. Jessica felt more and more that she was in the way.

"Look . . ." she said, getting to her feet. She still

had her eyes on her parents and Elizabeth, who didn't seem—thank heavens—to have spotted her yet. "I'm going to go get a Coke. Can I bring something back for you guys?"

"Let me come with you," Josh said, his eyes on Anita. It was obvious he was happier right where he was.

"No, I'll just be a minute," Jessica assured him. She gave Anita a little smile to show that she understood completely. At this point all she cared about, anyway, was saving face and getting out of this whole mess as gracefully as possible.

But she'd barely gotten three feet away when Steven hurried after her. "Would you mind telling me what on earth is going on?" he cried. "Jessica, since when do you tell Mom and Dad that you're going away for the weekend and then end up out with some guy four years older than you?"

Jessica's eyes filled with tears. "Don't yell at me," she begged him. "Steven, I'm in a terrible mess. I lied to Mom and Dad, I lied to you, I lied to everyone. I can't even remember whom I told what."

Steven put his arm around her, looking back uneasily at the spot where Megan, Josh, and Anita were engrossed in conversation. "OK, listen," he said. "I'm going along with your story and acting as if I'd never met you before tonight. We can talk about this later. Just make sure Mom and Dad don't see you. Something tells me they're not going to be half as understanding as I'm being."

"Thank you," Jessica said gratefully, dashing the tears from her eyes.

"Look," Steven added, "I don't want to make your life any more miserable than it already is. But I have the feeling that Anita and Josh . . ."

"I know, I know," Jessica said. "It's obvious. But I couldn't care less. Steven, all I want is to get out of this whole mess without Mom and Dad killing me—and without making a total jerk out of myself." Her blue-green eyes were big and shiny with tears. "I don't want Josh to know I was lying when I told him I was fourteen."

Steven shook his head. "OK," he said. "But I still think it'll be a miracle if you can pull it off."

Jessica shot him a look as she hurried off. He wasn't being all that encouraging, but on the other hand she had to admit it was incredibly nice of him not to tell the others on her. She would never in a million years have guessed he'd be so supportive in a crisis.

Jessica was walking so quickly and thinking so hard that she wasn't looking where she was going. She turned abruptly to look back at the group and knocked smack into the girl next to her, sending her cup of soda flying. "Sorry!" Jessica cried, turning to stare into the incredulous eyes of her twin.

"Jessica!" Elizabeth cried. "What on earth—"

Jessica's eyes were as big as saucers. "Uh, listen, I-I can explain," she stammered.

Elizabeth wiped soda off her sleeve with one

hand, her expression changing from astonishment to alarm. "Don't," she said urgently. "Mom and Dad are right behind me. You'd better get out of here as fast as possible unless you've got a really good reason for not being at Kerry's cabin."

Jessica didn't respond. Instead she turned and fled. But where should she go? What if her mother went to the ladies' room? What if her father . . . It was all such a mess. Jessica had no idea where to hide. She just wished she were back at home in her own bedroom and it were yesterday. She'd have time to rethink this whole mess and keep it from ever happening.

One thing was for sure. She was never going to lie about her age again. One tiny little fib had turned into such a complicated network of lies that she couldn't even imagine how to escape anymore.

Head hanging, Jessica walked slowly back to her seat. She hadn't even managed to buy herself a soda. And now it was time to go back and suffer through the second half of what—under ordinary circumstances—was her very favorite circus!

# Ten

◇

When Jessica got back to her seat she knew some-thing had changed between Josh and Anita. They both looked incredibly happy, and there was a kind of shyness and embarrassment in the way they looked at her that made the whole thing even more obvious. Good, Jessica thought. At least this part of the evening had gone the way she'd hoped it would. Now she could play the martyr and get out of there looking heroic, instead of foolish.

"Josh," she said, "can I talk to you for a minute—alone?"

Josh looked uneasily at Anita. "I'll see you later," he said, looking as if it were going to kill him to be separated from her for more than two seconds.

"Don't leave, Anita," Jessica admonished. "Just let me talk to Josh for a minute."

The two made their way through the crowd to a quiet corner. "Listen, Josh, I know what's going on," Jessica began. "It's obvious how much you want to be with Anita. And the truth is, I have a headache. Wouldn't it be simplest if I just went home now so you two could enjoy the rest of the circus together?"

Josh stared at her. "I'm not letting you go home alone." He reddened slightly. "It's true that I still like Anita—a lot. I'm really sorry to have gotten you mixed up in all this, Jessica. I guess I thought she and I were through when we really weren't. But that doesn't mean I'm going to let you disappear! I happen to be having a really good time with you. You're a really nice girl." He patted her arm awkwardly. "I feel bad enough about things as it is. Don't make me feel worse by disappearing."

*Darn*, Jessica thought. So much for her graceful exit.

"We'll have to get together and have lunch this week at school," Josh was saying. Jessica followed him miserably back to their seats. This was obviously his way of letting her down easily, trying to show her that they would still be friends. Fat chance, she was thinking. How were they going to get together in school when she wasn't even in high school yet?

The rest of the evening passed in a blur. She was so tired and confused that she barely appreciated the wonderful finale, when the woman in white was fired out of the big cannon. She just felt numb and dazed, and she was incredibly grateful when the lights came on again and Josh helped her on with her jacket. Anita and Diane had gone back to their seats for the second half, and if Josh had made any plans to meet Anita later, he didn't mention them. In fact, he was being the perfect gentleman. Jessica had to hand it to him.

Maybe this whole predicament wasn't that awful. After all, she *had* gotten to see the circus, even if she hadn't been able to enjoy it as much as usual. And even if Josh clearly wasn't interested in her as anything but a friend, she'd had the thrill of two real dates with him. More important, he had actually believed she was fourteen. Not once had he suspected that she was still only in middle school. Jessica was trying her hardest to console herself as they discussed where to go next. In fact, she was so deep in thought that she didn't even realize the Wakefields were walking straight toward them. She heard her father's voice before she saw him. "Steven! Steven!" he was calling, waving around a program. "Wait a minute!"

Jessica shoved her hands in her pockets, her heart pounding wildly. This was it. She'd been caught.

Her parents were hurrying over now, looking pleased to have spotted their son and eager to meet his new girlfriend. It was at least a full moment before they took in the fact that Jessica was by his side.

"Jess—" Mrs. Wakefield stammered, staring at her.

"Jessica!" Mr. Wakefield cried. "What on earth are you doing here? You're supposed to be at Kerry Glenn's cabin!"

"Hey," Josh said, staring at Elizabeth and then at Jessica, "you didn't tell me that you were part of a matched set!"

Jessica backed up uneasily, staring at her parents. "I—uh, I can explain everything later. At home," she said. This was exactly what she'd been dreading. Any minute Josh was going to find out the truth.

"Um, maybe we'd better make some introductions here," Steven said. "Megan, Josh, these are my parents and my sister, Elizabeth."

Josh started to shake Mr. Wakefield's hand before it dawned on him what Steven had just said. "Your sister!" he cried, staring at Elizabeth. He turned back to Jessica, his face confused. "But then what . . ." He shook his head, as if trying to clear it. "Are you trying to tell me you and Jessica are brother and sister? But I thought you said. . . . What's going on here?"

"That," Mr. Wakefield said, crossing his arms, "is exactly what we'd all like to know."

"Dad," Jessica said, her voice quavering, "can't we talk at home? Please?"

"Listen, Dad," Steven said, interceding on her behalf, "Jessica is okay. She's with me. Let me bring her home, and we can talk about this then." He gestured at the crowds around them. "Please, it's too noisy here. I promise she'll be fine."

Mrs. Wakefield looked incredibly distraught. "But what about Kerry?" she demanded.

"Mom, I'll explain everything," Jessica said in a low voice. She felt the last vestiges of her sophistication crumbling. Josh must think she was the biggest baby he'd ever met. It was so embarrassing—running into her parents and having them grill her in front of him!

The Wakefields exchanged glances. "OK," Mrs. Wakefield said. "We'll meet you at home."

Jessica knew she ought to be grateful, but by this point she was almost too miserable to care. All she wanted was to be back in her own house.

"OK," Josh said, once the four of them were in his car, driving back to the Wakefields' house. "Who wants to tell me what's going on here?"

"I'm Steven's sister," Jessica said dully.

"And you have a twin," Josh prompted.

Jessica nodded. "That's Elizabeth. We were born exactly four minutes apart."

"But if Steven's a freshman, and you and your twin are freshmen, what does that make you? Triplets? You sure don't look like Steven," Josh said.

Steven cleared his throat. "He's got a point, Jess," he said cheerfully. Jessica felt like murdering him.

"I'm not really a freshman," she said softly. She was slumped way down in her seat, so her voice didn't get very far.

"What?" Josh asked blankly.

"I'm not a freshman!" Jessica shrieked. "I lied about my age. I'm only twelve."

"You're only—" Josh stared at her. He put his foot on the brake as they came to a stop sign, his face incredulous. "You're kidding," he said. Megan didn't say a word, and Steven—even Steven—looked sympathetic. Jessica felt her eyes well up with tears. Josh turned bright red. "You mean to tell me that I've been . . . that you're only . . ." He looked incredibly embarrassed. The next minute embarrassment seemed to give way to anger. "Great," he muttered. "I guess that's what I get for taking people at their word."

Jessica felt terrible. "I'm really sorry," she said in a tiny voice.

Josh was quiet for a minute and then seemed to forget his anger. His face gradually cleared, and he almost seemed amused by the incident, rather than angry.

"Don't feel too bad," Josh said, patting her hand. "You want to hear a funny story? When I was thirteen I wanted to drive more than anything in the world. One day I took my father's car and just got in it and drove—all the way up to the mall. A cop stopped me, and I told him I was sixteen. I kept saying I was sixteen over and over again, even when they took me into the station and called my parents."

He patted her hand again.

Jessica pulled it away. She felt as if she were about three. "Yeah," she said dully. "Well, I'm really sorry, Josh."

"So that's why I could never find you at school," Josh mused.

Jessica stared out the window, her eyes aching. She couldn't wait to get out of the car. She didn't know which was worse—Josh being so darned *nice* about it, which made her feel as if *he* was *her* baby sister, or Steven's sympathetic look.

One thing was for sure. Her parents weren't going to be one bit nice or sympathetic. Something told her she was really going to be in for it when she got home.

"Just tell me one thing," Mr. Wakefield said, his arms crossed and a stern look on his face as he looked at Jessica across the kitchen table. "Did the Glenns ever invite you to their cabin this weekend or was that a lie, too?"

"Look," Jessica said, dashing the tears from her eyes, "I'm going to tell you the whole thing, from the very beginning. But you have to promise not to yell at me until I'm done, OK? Because I know how mad you are, and right now I'm so upset I'm afraid I'll cry if you interrupt!"

Elizabeth couldn't help thinking this was a great strategy on her twin's part. Mr. Wakefield looked softer right away, and Mrs. Wakefield looked almost—though not quite—sympathetic.

Taking a deep breath, Jessica proceeded to

launch into a detailed, though heavily edited, version of what had gone on with Josh for the past few weeks. She did everything she could to make herself seem as innocent as possible, insisting that she had had no idea how old Josh was until she'd already promised to go out with him that night. She didn't mention their prior date or the fact that she'd lied about her own age. But her tactic throughout was to admit—over and over again—how wrong she'd been.

"I really learned my lesson," she said mournfully, once she'd told them all she was willing to for the time being. "The thing is, you guys have always told us not to lie, and I know what I did was rotten and wrong. But I guess tonight I really found out how terrible it is to lie. One thing leads to another, and before you know what's happened you've turned everything into a real mess."

Elizabeth couldn't believe it. Only Jessica could do something really rotten and manage to reproach herself so much that she ended up sounding virtuous! It was truly obnoxious. And the worst part was that her parents seemed to be listening to—and *approving* of what Jessica said!

"I'm never going to tell another lie," Jessica added. "Not as long as I live."

"Well," Mrs. Wakefield said seriously, "if that's really true, then what you've been through is worth it. Because you're absolutely right, Jessica. One lie leads to another, and before you know it you've lied yourself into a terrible corner."

"That's true," Mr. Wakefield seconded. "Look, Jessica, what you've told us worries me for several reasons. First of all, it shows poor judgment. You had no business agreeing to spend time with someone—especially a boy, and a boy older than you are—whom we've never met. And to actually go out with him in a car without telling us was very bad judgment indeed. But that's only the first part of the problem. The next problem was that you lied to us about this weekend. Where were you last night if you weren't in the mountains with the Glenns?"

"Yes, and who was it who called me and said you were invited for the weekend?" Mrs. Wakefield added.

Jessica hung her head. The best thing to do was to admit the truth and be apologetic, she decided. "I was at Lila's. And it was Lila who called you, Mom. I put her up to it. In fact I had to beg her to do it."

A long silence followed this declaration.

"I just don't know what to say, Jessica," Mr. Wakefield said, looking sadly at her. "I can't remember ever being so disappointed in you. It's a horrible feeling to think that I can't trust you. But I'm afraid I can't. You've really let me down."

Mrs. Wakefield looked at Jessica, her blue eyes grave. "I wish I knew what kind of punishment would be best," she said. "It seems to me that you've proven that we can't trust you. My feeling is that you should be grounded for the next two weeks. Other than going to school, I don't want you to leave this house, for anything."

"I agree," Mr. Wakefield said. "This is far too serious to go unpunished, Jessica."

Jessica, her head hanging, waited for them to finish. She couldn't believe it. *Grounded!* Suddenly all the things she wanted to do in the next two weeks came to her.

"I'm really sorry," she said again. She meant it, too. She couldn't believe that she'd gone through all this torture for Josh. And all so that he and Anita could discover how much they were still in love! "I promise I'll never disappoint you like this again." *Please*, she thought. *Make them change their minds about grounding me.* But her parents looked as firm as she'd ever seen them.

No one said anything for a long time. Then Jessica cleared her throat. "Can I call Lila and tell her that I'm not going to be there tonight so she doesn't worry?"

Her parents nodded, and Jessica—breathing a sigh of relief now that she was free to escape from their accusing gazes—hurried out of the room.

What a disastrous night, she thought sorrowfully. She climbed the stairs at breakneck speed, pulled the phone into her room, and closed the door behind her with a small thud. She threw herself face-down on her bed and tried to conjure up one good memory from the evening. But she couldn't. It had been rotten from beginning to end. Sighing heavily, she dialed Lila's number.

"Hey! How's everything going? Are you madly in love?" Lila demanded eagerly.

"Lila," Jessica said heavily, "I'm not coming back tonight. So don't wait up for me."

"What?" Lila shrieked. "Jessica, what are you talking about? You're not going to do something crazy, are you?"

"I'm at home, Lila," Jessica said flatly. "It's kind of hard to explain right now, but Josh and I sort of bumped into my whole family tonight. To make a long story short, they found out. So here I am," she concluded.

"Oh, no," Lila moaned. "How did you run into your family? I can't believe it. And I was sitting here all night imagining you having the time of your life!"

Jessica stared glumly at the telephone. "Tonight," she said dramatically, "was one of the worst nights I've ever had. And to top the whole thing off, I barely even got to enjoy the circus."

"What circus? You don't mean Josh took you to the circus!" Lila cried. "What's romantic about a circus?"

Despite herself Jessica was beginning to see a tiny glimmer of amusement in the situation. "Lila," she said, twisting the phone cord around her finger, "the circus wasn't the only thing that was unromantic. If you're ready for it, I can describe an evening that would win any unromantic competition hands down!"

And with that, she proceeded to describe the evening to Lila in perfect detail—starting with the minute she realized they were driving back to her own house to pick up Megan's date!

# Eleven

◇

Elizabeth had to hand it to Jessica. That girl really knew how to come out of a crisis looking like a hero! By noon on Monday it seemed as if everyone at school knew all about Jessica's wild romance with Josh. And from the stories that were spreading around, Jessica was nothing short of incredible. The rumor was that Jessica had fallen madly in love with a handsome, popular junior; that they'd dated secretly for weeks before getting caught; and that Jessica had nobly given Josh up so that he could go back to his old girlfriend. Caroline Pearce was instrumental in spreading most of the stories, but the Unicorns helped, too. Ellen Riteman and Lila followed Jessica around all day, linking arms and assuring her over and over again that they'd do their best to cheer her up.

In fact, all the Unicorns seemed to be treating Jessica with new respect. Most of them had never been on a real date—in a *car*—and no one had ever been kissed by a sixteen-year-old. They all wanted to hear about her disastrous date over and over again. Actually Jessica was enjoying being a minor celebrity. It almost made up for the fact that her parents had grounded her for the next two weeks to punish her for having lied and used bad judgment.

"You can't be grounded," Ellen Riteman pointed out at lunch, taking a ham sandwich out of her bag and unwrapping it. "Kimberly Haver is having a big birthday party two weeks from Friday. Everyone's coming! It's going to be one of the biggest parties this whole year."

Jessica wrinkled her brow. "My parents are pretty mad," she said unhappily. "Believe me, I don't want to be grounded, either. But I don't really see how I can talk them out of it."

"If I know you, Jess, you'll come up with a plan," Ellen said, taking a bite of her sandwich.

"I want to hear more about Josh," Lila said eagerly. "When did you last talk to him?"

"He called last night, just to see how I was doing. He's really a nice guy," Jessica mused. "But he's definitely getting back together with Anita. He told me"—she grimaced—"that I was what brought them back together. Isn't that sickening?"

"I think it's incredibly romantic." Lila sighed.

"Anyway, he said he's going to tell all his cute friends to look out for me—in another year or two!" Jessica shook her head. "I bet I'll still be grounded by then."

Everyone laughed. But Ellen still believed Jessica would get out of being punished. With Jessica, it was just a question of how!

Elizabeth looked with interest at the sign posted on the bulletin board outside the school office. "Hey," she said to Tom McKay, who was standing next to her, "there's going to be a statewide essay contest. Look! There's a first prize of a hundred dollars. It would be great to win something like that, wouldn't it?"

Tom, one of the cutest and most popular boys in the sixth-grade class, looked at the sign with interest. "I should talk my brother into entering," he said. "Dylan is a really great writer."

Elizabeth was intrigued. She loved to write herself, and she was always interested in learning about classmates who shared her passion. She didn't know Tom's older brother Dylan very well. It had always seemed to her that Tom was the more outstanding of the two in every way. Tom was a great athlete, whereas Dylan was just average at sports. Tom got good grades and had lots of friends, while Dylan—who got decent grades—was fairly shy and spent a lot of time alone. Everyone liked and knew

Tom, and Dylan . . . well, Dylan was just kind of *there*.

"Hey, Dylan!" Tom cried, waving at his brother as he crossed the hall several yards in front of them. "Come here! There's something I want to show you."

Dylan flicked his light brown hair out of his eyes and came over. He was a tall, slightly gangly seventh grader who looked slightly ill at ease, as if he'd gotten too tall too quickly. He smiled shyly at Elizabeth, then turned red and looked away. Elizabeth felt sorry for him, though she wasn't exactly sure why.

"Look at this. There's going to be a statewide essay competition," Tom said, pointing to the bulletin board.

Dylan flipped his hair back again, frowning. "So?"

"So you should enter," Tom said, slapping him on the back. "Come on, Dylan. You're a great writer!"

"Aw," Dylan muttered, "I could never win something like that. Forget it, Tom." And with a quick sideways glance at Elizabeth he turned and shuffled off down the hall. Tom stared after him, a look of consternation on his handsome face.

"What is it?" Elizabeth asked him.

"Oh, nothing," Tom said. But Elizabeth guessed he just didn't want to tell her what he was thinking. It was obvious he was worrying about his older brother.

*Is Elizabeth about to find herself in the middle of a feud between two brothers? Find out in Sweet Valley Twins #16, SECOND BEST.*

IT ALL STARTED WITH

## THE

# SWEET VALLEY TWINS

**F**or two years teenagers across the U.S. have been reading about Jessica and Elizabeth Wakefield and their High School friends in SWEET VALLEY HIGH books. Now in books created especially for you, author Francine Pascal introduces you to Jessica and Elizabeth when they were 12, facing the same problems with their folks and friends that you do.

# THE CLASS TRIP

## SWEET VALLEY TWINS SUPER EDITION #1

Join Jessica and Elizabeth in the very first SWEET VALLEY TWINS Super Edition—it's longer, can be read out of sequence, and is full of page-turning excitement!

The day of the big sixth-grade class trip to the Enchanted Forest is finally here! But Jessica and Elizabeth have a fight and spend the beginning of the trip arguing. When Elizabeth decides to make up, Jessica has disappeared. In a frantic search for her sister, Elizabeth finds herself in a series of dangerous and exciting Alice In Wonderland-type of adventures.

☐ 15588-1   $2.95/$3.50 in Canada

Buy them at your local bookstore or use this page to order.

------------------------------------------------